SHARING
What's Real

KENZIE BRAYNE

HAVEN VALLEY HIGH #3

SHARING
What's Real

MORLEY

BOOKS

1

Lauren

FOR THE SECOND time in five minutes, I stared open-mouthed at Chloe and Nate kissing against my kitchen counter. The fiery anger that caused me to scream at them the first time had dissipated, leaving behind a mix of disbelief and confusion.

"Okay, okay, we get the idea," Emma said, causing Chloe and Nate to separate and reveal bashful grins. "Why don't you guys all go downstairs? Lauren and I will be with you in a minute."

Emma had addressed everyone in the room with more authority than usual. It wasn't all that subtle, but hopefully no one else realized it was because she wanted to talk to me alone.

I glanced at Jason. He was standing to the side with a relieved smile plastered across his face. As if feeling my eyes on him, he met my gaze, and I forgot how to breathe.

The eye contact with Jason only lasted a second before he turned away and left the kitchen with the rest of our friends.

Emma waited until we heard the basement door close

before she grabbed hold of me, squeezing tight. "I can't believe it. Can you believe it?"

No. Everything I thought I knew was a lie, and now the truth was out—they'd confessed everything.

Emma released me, stepping back to observe my reaction. But there was none.

"Lauren? Are you in shock or something? This is huge. You understand what this means?" Her grin was enormous.

I nodded, but something about my vacant expression must have made Emma want to explain it again anyway.

"They were faking! This whole time. That means Jason is single. There was never anything between him and Chloe. Do you hear me? He's available. It's what you've been waiting for. There's nothing stopping you now!"

Oh, how I wished that was true, but there was still one thing stopping me, and it was the same thing as always—me.

I'd fallen hard for one of my best friends, but it was all one-sided. Jason didn't have a clue how I felt, and I could never bring myself to tell him. I couldn't risk the rejection, risk losing our friendship.

"Well? What do you have to say?" Emma was still waiting for a reaction, but her excited expression was slowly morphing into a disheartened frown.

"I need to think about it."

Emma groaned. "What's to think about? You should act now, before you talk yourself out of it. Tell him how you feel. What's the point of being impulsive if you freeze up when it matters? Why don't I go downstairs and send Jason back up?" She gave me a hopeful smile.

"No!" Her threat jolted me from my daze. "I'm not ready

to talk to him." I needed to be ready. I wouldn't let Emma pressure me.

Her face fell in disappointment. She wasn't usually a pushy person, but after witnessing my heartbreak on the first day of school when I found out Jason had a girlfriend, I couldn't blame her for wanting me to seize this second chance.

"Well, okay." Emma's frown deepened. "Let's talk about it later?"

I nodded. I wanted to pretend like this was a regular Sunday night movie night at my house. Just hanging out with friends, without any life-shattering revelations.

I still needed to digest the new information, and ninety-plus minutes of sitting in darkness would provide that opportunity, so I followed Emma down to my basement—our home theater.

We had two couches facing the gigantic projector screen, both angled in toward each other. My usual seat was next to Jason on the three-seater, but tonight, with the inclusion of Nate sprawled out on the other side of Chloe, that couch was looking full.

Instead, I followed Emma to the two-seater. She always sat close enough to her boyfriend, Kai, that she was practically on top of him anyway, so I would have plenty of space. It made more sense for me to sit here, and even though I always preferred to be close to Jason, the distance might help me think clearly.

"Your movie room is awesome," Nate said with a smile when I sat down.

"Thanks."

I loved showing it off. My parents had converted the entire basement and installed a 4k projector along with 7.1 surround sound. They'd paid extra for insulation, so even during the noisiest action sequences, you couldn't hear a peep upstairs. Plus, everything was smart. It was all connected, even the room's lighting, so I had complete control from my phone.

"Everyone ready?" I asked, before starting the movie.

I'd chosen a comedy for tonight. It was Nate's first time joining us, and although I didn't know him well, when I asked, Kai and Emma assured me he'd enjoy comedy the most.

Their recommendation was spot on, since judging from his boisterous laughter, Nate was having a fun time. Although his attention seemed to be as much on Chloe as on the screen.

I sighed, wishing one day Jason would look at me that way. My eyes shifted to him, but only for a second, so he wouldn't catch me staring. Jason looked cool, calm, and collected, like always. His tousled blond hair was crying out for me to ruffle it up with my fingers. Not that I'd ever dare. From just a quick glance, I could tell he was in a great mood.

Jason's single now. It was all an act.

The movie finished before I was ready, and the rolling credits brought me back to reality. Even though I'd intended to use the movie's full runtime to think things through, to make a plan, my mind had accomplished nothing.

Unless fantasizing about Jason was an accomplishment? In which case, I was an overachiever. But in my dreams I was strong and brave, and it was easy to do everything I feared in real life. Because in my dreams he wanted me too.

"Good choice tonight." Jason broke the silence. He was always first to offer an opinion on my movie selection, and I loved how often I could successfully predict what he would say.

Chloe nodded her agreement, then looked over at me,

Emma, and Kai. "Thank you all for being so understanding with everything. It makes me a lot less nervous about school tomorrow."

She hadn't shared all the details, but Chloe's family had lost their wealth. She'd had some misguided belief that people would judge her for it, and it was her fear of anyone finding out that had prompted the crazy plan of a fake relationship. Jason had been trying to help her, because he'd always help anyone in need.

I cringed, remembering how I'd screamed at Chloe when I walked in on her kissing Nate earlier tonight, before they'd confessed the truth. Thinking she was betraying Jason, I'd seen red.

"I'm sorry for yelling at you earlier," I said.

"No worries. You were just being protective of Jason. He's lucky to have you in his corner." Chloe glanced over at him as she spoke, but Jason wasn't looking at her. He was focused on me, giving me one of his gorgeous smiles.

My heart skipped a beat as I briefly met his hazel eyes before shifting my gaze away. He always had an effect on me, but something had changed. I didn't normally feel this nervous.

"We should probably get going," Emma said, extricating herself from Kai's vice-like grip, then standing up.

I'd expected Emma to want to stay behind so we could continue our conversation, but rushing off made more sense. She'd try to engineer it so I was left alone with Jason. It was a wasted effort on her part though, because I still had no clue what to say to him, and I was definitely not ready to blurt out my feelings tonight.

"Yeah, I should head to bed," I said, even though it was

way too early for that excuse to be believable. "I'm exhausted. Far too much excitement for one day." I did my best to look tired, only stopping short of a fake yawn, which would have made it obvious I was lying.

Jason took the hint and stood up with the others. Emma glared at me, her face unable to hide her disappointment, but I averted my gaze down to the cartoon space rockets printed on the carpet.

Following my friends up the stairs out of the basement, I kept my head low as I steered them to the front door and made sure they all left together.

After giving them a friendly wave goodbye, I slammed the door shut and took in a deep breath. Getting rid of them so fast was unusual, but I needed space. My head was too cloudy.

Tonight had been a blur. My mind still hadn't processed the influx of information, and I needed to think it over alone. I wouldn't have *that conversation* with Jason until I knew what to say. But I did know one thing.

This changed everything. It granted me a second chance, and I wasn't going to waste it.

2

Jason

I PULLED my car up outside Lauren's house. With Chloe riding to school with Nate, my travel time had reduced drastically. Plus, Emma was getting a ride with Kai today, so, for the first time in what felt like an eternity, it would be just me and Lauren in the car for the drive to school.

I was glad. At least I thought I was.

Out of everyone, I'd been dying to confess the truth to Lauren the most. Last night, she hardly looked at me. I wanted a chance to explain, to apologize for lying to her for so long. And even though it wouldn't make a difference to Lauren, I wanted to clarify that there was never anything between me and Chloe.

I reached for my phone and sent her a message.

JASON

Running early today. I'm outside

Lauren didn't keep me waiting for long.

"Hey." She greeted me with a smile as she slid into the car. "It's good to be back in the front."

I returned her smile. "What are you going to do with all the extra legroom?"

My eyes trailed over Lauren's long, denim-clad legs, which she stretched out in front of her.

"Guess I'll just enjoy it while I can."

"While you can?" My eyes returned to her face, and I did my best not to stare. It was always a struggle with Lauren though, because she was beautiful. Most people focused on her hair. It was dark brown, long, thick, and lustrous. It was her defining feature, although from the amount she complained, I wasn't sure it was worth it. She'd still look amazing even if she shaved it all off, and I was much more interested in those warm caramel eyes.

Lauren had no idea how I felt about her, and even though I'd been tempted to cross that invisible friend barrier on more than one occasion, I'd be a fool to mess up what we had. Especially when she didn't feel the same.

Although, what we had right now wasn't as good as it had been. We'd been spending far less time together than we used to, and I was hoping things would pick up again. That she might have missed me as much as I missed her.

Lauren shrugged, but her meaning wasn't lost on me. Did she really think I'd be getting a new girlfriend any time soon?

"Make yourself at home." I returned my eyes to the road ahead and started the engine. The front seat was hers for as long as she wanted.

"So, will I be seeing more of you now?" she asked.

"You can count on it."

"Good. Your fake girlfriend took up all of your time."

She wasn't wrong. I'd spent a lot of time driving Chloe around since she'd been forced to sell her car.

I never expected our fake relationship to last for so long. Sometimes I wished I'd never even offered at all, but Chloe had been sobbing in my car and I couldn't just sit back and watch her cry without at least trying to help.

What I thought would be two weeks had turned into three months, and now I was more than ready to get my old life back. Not that things with Chloe had been bad; we'd had some fun, and I now considered her one of my closest friends. But I'd put my real life on hold and lied to everyone.

I opened my mouth to apologize, but Lauren kept talking. "I missed you."

"You did?" My voice did nothing to hide how happy that made me. "You still saw me plenty."

"Not really. You stopped sitting with us at lunch. I can't even remember the last time you came over for a monster movie, and by the way, I now have a massive backlog. Plus, you never come over to the house anymore. Even my dad's been saying how much he misses you."

I chuckled at that. I got on well with Keith, and it was true I hadn't seen him much in the past few months.

"Let's fix that then. Tell me about this backlog?"

Lauren loved watching low-budget monster movies, and while I couldn't say I shared her passion for them, I enjoyed watching them with her. The best thing was that it was always just the two of us, mostly because no one else would humor her and tolerate the movies. But I got to spend an evening alone with Lauren, and that was worth it.

"The Mega Monster Movie Extravaganza Festival has made all this year's nominees available for streaming. I really want to watch as many as possible before the festival."

"The Mega Monster Movie Extravaganza Festival?" I repeated slowly. "Did you tell me about that? When is it?"

"It's in February. The timing fits perfectly with mid-winter break. I must have mentioned it."

I didn't think she had. But we were only just into December, so there was plenty of time to plan.

"Did you already get tickets?" I asked.

"No. Why? Would you want to go?" Her jaw dropped.

"Sure, I mean, I figured you'd want to?" I glanced over at Lauren, unsure why she looked so surprised.

"Well, of course, I'd love to. But I didn't think—"

"Book it then," I interrupted her. "I'll go with you."

She grinned. "But you haven't even asked where it is."

"Where is it?"

"It's in Las Vegas." She clenched her teeth together, but the eagerness was still in her eyes. I wasn't sure how much fun Las Vegas was for under 21s, but I'd go anywhere with Lauren.

"We can go to Vegas." I stole another glance at her, and she looked about ready to explode from excitement. "It should be easy to find a flight."

She nodded with enthusiasm, and I felt a surge of pride that I was the one to put that joyful expression on her face.

"I should check with my parents before booking anything." She pulled out her phone and started typing out a message, although I was sure they'd say yes. I'd check with Mom later but couldn't imagine a problem there either.

Lauren received a reply almost instantly, and she snickered as she read it. "That's approval from my parents."

"What's so funny?"

"My dad suggested we should let Elvis marry us." She

smiled at me as she rolled her eyes, and my heart skipped a beat.

Keith had made plenty of jokes over the years about the two of us getting married, but while Lauren seemed to find her dad amusing, I found it uncomfortable. Because it hit too close to home. I was in no rush to settle down, but I could totally imagine marrying Lauren one day.

Not in Vegas in February, but one day in the very, very distant future.

Lauren returned her attention to her phone. "So, I should go ahead and book?" Her huge grin was back.

"Yeah. These things have different packages, don't they?"

I'd been so caught up in Lauren's excitement, I was only now thinking about how much this trip would cost. I'd saved up some money from waiting tables over the summer, but this could turn into an expensive trip.

"I'll see," Lauren said, and I waited while she loaded up the website. She paused before letting out a long sigh. "It's sold out."

"Completely sold out? Don't they have some super-expensive VIP package that never sells out?" Not that I could afford super-expensive, but if it was the only option, I'd find a way.

"They did have one. But then it sold out." She sighed again. "Guess we were too slow. Never mind."

I couldn't bear the disappointment in her voice.

"I'm so sorry," I said as the guilt took hold.

"Not your fault, but thanks for offering to come with me. That means a lot."

I didn't have a response for her, because I felt responsible. If she'd mentioned it sooner, we would've gotten tickets in time. And she would have mentioned it sooner if things had been normal, if I hadn't been pretending to date Chloe.

I let out my own disappointed sigh. "We can still watch the nominees?"

"Yeah, that'll keep us busy. We should get started right away. Are you free at all this week?"

I nodded. My social calendar was completely open for the foreseeable future. "I'm free all week. So how about we make a start tomorrow? And pick a good one, or I might not be back for the rest."

"Hey, they'll all be good." She gave me a gentle punch on the arm and then laughed. "Tomorrow works for me. And we need to get together with Emma and Kai at some point. Do some planning for our road trip, assuming you still want to come along?"

"Yeah, of course."

Lauren and Emma were planning an epic road trip for after graduation. This was the first I'd heard about Kai going too, but I didn't want to mention it and draw any more attention to how much I'd missed.

It made sense they'd invite Kai. He and Emma were joined at the hip. But traveling with a couple changed the group dynamic, unless by then...

"What are you going to tell people at school about you and Chloe?" Lauren pulled me out of my thoughts and back to the harsh reality of the day.

Today would be a big deal for Chloe. She was anxious about admitting the truth. That her family had lost a lot of money and she was no longer the spoiled rich girl people believed her to be.

"It might be unconventional, but we've decided to go with the truth," I said.

I didn't know how anyone would react to that, but I needed to brace myself for ridicule. I'd never had an actual girlfriend, only a fake one, and by the end of the day, everyone would know our relationship had been a sham.

"You know there was never anything between us, don't you?" I added. "Our entire relationship was pretend. Chloe's just a friend."

Lauren's face twisted with slight confusion, as if she was wondering why I was repeating this information that she'd already been told.

In the beginning, she'd hated the idea of me with Chloe and didn't hide it well. I'd foolishly hoped she might be jealous, but it was probably just shock. And after a rocky beginning, she got used to us dating almost too fast, welcoming Chloe into our friendship group.

For the rest of the ride to school, neither of us said anything else about my relationship with Chloe. Instead, Lauren talked me through the list of nominees for the festival. It sounded like there were a lot, and it would take us many evenings to catch up. But I didn't mind. I didn't mind at all.

3

Lauren

PEOPLE WERE TALKING. Mostly about Chloe. But also about Jason. By the time I sat down for lunch with Emma and Kai, I was beyond worried.

The way Chloe told her story, it was as if Jason had swooped in and rescued her. She was talking him up, gushing over him, and making him sound positively heroic. I wanted to tell her to stop, but I couldn't. He deserved the credit he was getting.

I knew exactly what Jason was like. That he was the kind of guy who would go out of his way to help others and would always put them first. Now the rest of the girls at school were finding out too, and I hated it.

I'd been fielding questions all morning. They wanted to know everything about him, but I didn't want to share any of my insider information. I wanted to keep it, and him, all to myself.

"You doing okay?" Emma asked me. "Jason sure is getting a lot of attention today."

That was putting it mildly. For every girl who came to ask me questions, two were talking to him directly.

I looked up from my fries to where Jason waited in line for food. As expected, he was talking with a couple of flirtatious girls, making my jealousy flare.

Unsure what to say, I didn't answer Emma and instead just nodded. Besides, Kai was here, and I wasn't going to talk about my feelings for Jason in front of anyone else.

"Is he going to sit with us today?" she asked.

I shrugged.

Emma gave me a sympathetic smile, but possibly sensing she wouldn't get much conversation out of me, she turned back to Kai.

Jason looked so smiley and happy, like he was relishing the attention. One of the girls he was talking with leaned over far too close, totally invading his personal bubble, but Jason didn't object or try to back away.

I hadn't predicted this, and suddenly the need to confess my feelings felt desperate. I thought I'd lost him forever when he started dating Chloe. It was going to happen again. I just knew it. But this time it would be for real, and it might already be too late. He could already have a date lined up.

My stomach churned, and I pushed away the rest of my lunch. A few minutes later, Jason joined us at our table.

"Somebody's popular today," Emma teased, twirling some of her long blonde hair around her finger.

Jason laughed. "It's crazy. People have been staring at me all day. I don't know what Chloe's been telling them, but she must be embellishing the truth. I don't know how else to explain all this interest."

"Have you been collecting phone numbers?" Kai asked.

Jason puffed his cheeks before blowing out a long breath. "Something like that, plus I even had a proposition earlier." He cringed a little.

"What did you say?" Emma asked, unable to hide her shock as she flicked her eyes to me.

"I said no, of course. What do you think I'm like?" Jason pretended to be appalled, but he was smiling too much for it to be convincing.

Emma frowned. "Ignore those girls, Jason. Half of them probably didn't know you existed last week. And they'll have forgotten about you by tomorrow."

Emma was only trying to help me, but she was wrong.

The girls wouldn't forget so easily. Jason was a catch, and the more people that knew it, the more determined they would be. For some girls, it was almost a competitive sport. Jason was the hot property right now. They'd want to be first in line to date him, and to tell everyone that this time, he wasn't faking.

Jason let out a light chuckle. "I'll try not to be offended by that."

"You know what I mean. Wouldn't you rather date someone who likes you for you, not just because Chloe says you're her hero?"

Jason's brow furrowed. "Don't worry, Emma. I can see what's going on. It's only a bit of fun. Besides, I promised Lauren we'd catch up on all her monster movies. I don't know when I'd find time for dating."

Jason flashed me a smile, and it almost made everything better. But the worry was still there, festering in my gut.

EMMA PULLED me aside after we left the cafeteria, sending Kai on his way and promising to catch up with him later. We already lost Jason halfway through lunch, when Chloe called him over to her table, so now Emma and I were alone for the first time all day.

"Why didn't you tell him this morning?" Emma had an accusatory tone.

"In the car? Did you seriously expect me to?"

"I guess not." Her voice softened. "But I hoped. I just don't want you to miss this opportunity. I know you'd never forgive yourself. Don't you remember how you felt on the first day of school?"

That wasn't something I'd ever be able to forget. Jason had blindsided me, announcing from nowhere that he and Chloe were dating. It had felt as if my entire universe had caved in. Before then, I'd been complacent, waiting for the perfect moment to confess my feelings. Searching for clues, needing to find signs he might feel the same before putting my heart on the line.

"Look, Lauren. I'm sorry I'm being so pushy, but I know you'll regret it forever if you don't do anything, if you don't at least try. And now it looks like you have competition."

I nodded. She was right. "I know. I'm going to tell him."

"You are? You mean it?"

I nodded again, and my heart started pounding from nervous excitement just at the thought. Emma grinned at me, and she was no doubt about to question me further, but before she had a chance, Jason stepped out of the cafeteria with Chloe and Nate.

"Hey guys," Chloe greeted us with a broad smile. "Were you waiting for Jason?"

"We were just talking," Emma answered. "How are you doing today? It looks like things are going well?"

"It's so much better than I expected. Everyone has been really nice. I don't know what I was so worried about. And it helps that most of the attention is going on this one." She slid her arm around Jason, squeezing herself against his side in a half hug.

I stopped breathing. That was more affection than I'd ever seen between them, even when they were pretending to be in love. They'd held hands a lot, but never anything more.

I'd found it odd, but had been relieved, not wanting to see Jason getting too cozy with another girl. And it was probably only because of their lack of obvious intimacy that I was able to make friends with Chloe. If they'd been touching or kissing, I would've been too jealous. Just like now, despite knowing it meant nothing.

"Hey," Nate objected, then pulled Chloe away from Jason and back into him, wrapping both his arms around her.

Chloe laughed, then tilted her head to smile up at Nate, holding that pose for what felt to me like an awkwardly long time.

"Okay, well, I guess we should get going." Emma screwed up her face a little as she watched them. "I'm so glad things are going well, Chloe."

"Thanks." Chloe broke eye contact with Nate. "Is anyone going the same direction as Jason? I think he could use a body-guard today."

Jason shook his head at her. "I'm sure I'll survive. Catch you guys later."

He turned to leave, and I couldn't stop myself from watching him walk away.

"Did you notice how the girls have been fawning over him today?" Chloe asked. "I don't think it'll be long before he has a new girlfriend. A real one."

I clenched my teeth together. She was the one inviting attention to him. Attention he didn't ask for.

"You think so?" Emma asked. "I don't think he'd go for one of those girls. Jason should be with someone who actually knows him. Like we do."

"I agree. Someone who would make him truly happy. But she'll need to make a move soon, before he gets snapped up by someone else." Chloe shot me a glance, and when her eyes met mine, all I wanted to do was curl up into a little ball.

She was talking right at me. Did Chloe know how I felt about Jason? I'd obviously never told her, but maybe I didn't hide it as well as I thought.

"I'd like to see that happen," Emma said. "Jason deserves to be happy."

Chloe nodded intently, but I couldn't stay to listen. Reeling from the thought that Chloe knew my secret, I muttered my goodbyes and rushed away.

"DID YOU GET YOUR CONVENTION TICKETS?" Dad asked over dinner.

I finished chewing my mouthful of vegetables before answering him. "No. It was sold out."

"Oh, sweetie. I'm so sorry," Mom said. "That would have been such a fun trip."

I shrugged in response, not wanting her to make a big deal out of it, to feel the need to comfort me like I knew she would.

"It doesn't matter. It's my own fault for not telling Jason about it sooner."

"Why didn't you?" she asked.

"I thought about it. But he was dating Chloe, so suggesting we went away for a few days together felt wrong. Like it wasn't my place."

Dad dropped his fork onto his plate, making a loud clattering noise. "He *was* dating Chloe? Does that mean he's finally come to his senses?"

My entire family knew how I felt about Jason. It wasn't as if I'd sat them down and poured my heart out, but somehow they could tell. I didn't bother to deny it. They knew me too well.

And mostly, I was fine with them knowing, because they loved Jason too. They liked to tease us, especially Dad. But Jason thought Dad was just joking around, not realizing that even though he was in no hurry to marry off his youngest daughter, deep down he was rooting for us.

I smiled. The same hopeful smile that kept breaking out all day in between the fits of worry. "I was meaning to tell you about that."

Both my parents looked over at me, so I gave them the summary, explaining how Jason helped Chloe.

"What an idiot." Dad shook his head, almost in despair.

"Pretending to be in a relationship for over three months? What if you'd started dating someone else during that time?"

I gawked at him. As if that had been a possibility.

"Keith," Mom warned. "I don't think Lauren appreciates you calling her future husband an idiot."

I groaned. "He's not my future husband." I secretly hoped I was wrong.

"Future boyfriend then," Mom said. "But this is good news. We should celebrate."

Celebrate? My mom would jump at any opportunity.

"Let's go out for a special meal tomorrow. Invite Jason?"

I laughed, unsure how I would explain what we were celebrating to Jason. "Actually, I already have plans with him for tomorrow night."

"A date?" Mom raised an eyebrow.

"Seriously, Mom? He's just coming over to watch a movie. Assuming that's okay?" I didn't really need to ask permission. Jason was always welcome here. "You know Jason doesn't see me as more than a friend."

"He's an idiot," Dad said again.

"Keith," Mom gave him a second warning, causing Dad to hold his hands up in surrender.

"What? He's an eighteen-year-old boy. They're all idiots at that age."

Mom snickered. "And sometimes those teenage boys forget to grow up."

Dad playfully narrowed his eyes at her, and Mom winked in return.

My parents were goofballs, but they were the best. Excusing myself, I went to my room where, after finishing my homework, I spent the rest of the evening daydreaming and making plans for tomorrow night.

Deciding which movie we'd start with was easy. But planning out what to say was more of a challenge. The attention Jason received at school today served as a wake-up call. I couldn't do this on my schedule anymore. Emma was right. I wouldn't be able to bear it if he got another girlfriend before I'd built up the courage to confess my feelings.

So I was going to risk it all. I was going to tell him, and there was no time to waste. I would need to do it tomorrow.

4

Jason

"WELCOME BACK, SON." Keith pulled me inside the house, giving me a firm hug and clapping me on the back. It had been about a month since I last saw Keith, right after Halloween, but he was acting as if we'd been apart for years.

I didn't mind the physical contact, or when he affectionately called me *son*. We'd always been close, and with my deadbeat dad no longer in the picture, Keith had often felt like something of a father figure to me. Not that I'd ever told him.

"Thanks, Keith." I gave him a genuine smile.

Lauren's mom, Tina, also came to welcome me, stepping out from the kitchen. "Jason, sweetie, how are you doing?" She pulled me into a hug, holding on for far longer than Keith did before releasing me. "Lauren told us all about Chloe."

I scratched my neck, unsure of what to say. Did she tell them everything? She probably did. Lauren was close to her parents.

"A fake relationship?" Keith looked down his nose at me in mock disapproval. "I wouldn't put it past Emma, but I expected better of you." He was putting on some kind of strict headmaster voice that made me laugh.

Emma and Kai fell for each other while pretending to date for a bet—they'd fooled me from the start. But Keith was only joking about Emma. He liked to pretend she was a rebel, even though she was the most well-behaved person I knew.

"I'm glad it's over," I said, and Tina nodded in understanding.

"Well, it's good to see you." She gave me a warm smile. "But we know you aren't here to see us."

"Lauren! Your future husband's here!" Keith hollered up the stairs, making me wince.

Tina slapped him on the chest. "You know she doesn't like it when we call him that."

Keith shrugged and shot me a grin.

Lauren appeared at the top of the stairs. "Liam Redwood's here?"

Once halfway down, she stopped, then dropped her face in exaggerated disappointment as her eyes roamed over me.

I tightened my lips, trying to pretend I didn't find her funny. Liam Redwood was an actor in a series of her monster movies. He wore heavy makeup on-screen, completely unrecognizable. Lauren had joked that he was probably gorgeous underneath, so we looked him up, and well, Lauren stood by her initial assessment.

"Oh, hi, Jason. You're here too. Come on up."

Lauren turned to go back upstairs, so I jogged up to join her, and once we reached the top, Keith's voice rang out again. "Leave the door open!"

The comment caught me off guard. He'd never said

anything like that before, and so after stepping inside Lauren's room, I hesitated.

"Ignore him." Lauren pushed the door shut. "He's been getting excited now you're single again."

"Do we need to jump on the bed? Give him a real thrill?"

Lauren's eyes crinkled as she laughed at my joke. I loved making her laugh. It was one of my favorite things to do. I was such a sap.

She sat down on her bed, fluffing up her forest-green pillows and propping them against the headboard, before shuffling back so she was leaning against them.

Sometimes when we watched movies alone we'd be down in the basement, reclining on the couches. But mostly we'd stay in Lauren's room. If we were having snacks, she'd insist we sit on the floor. Otherwise, we would watch from the bed, relaxing back against the pillows, like today.

Joining her on the bed, I casually flung my arm over her shoulder. This was our movie watching position, and I didn't know how I got away with it. But Lauren always snuggled up against me, like it was perfectly normal. And in a way, it did feel normal. It felt natural.

But this was almost the only time we ever got this close physically, and it had always been a driving incentive in encouraging me to watch her terrible movies. If I'd tried to touch her like this in any other setting, she would've looked at me like I had three heads. But here, it wasn't a big deal, and we never mentioned it as anything unusual.

"What's our first movie?" I asked.

"It's called The Beast from Beneath the Deep. I've been looking forward to this one. Do you want to know what it's about, or go in blind?"

"Go in blind, of course. It's more fun to be surprised."

Lauren paused for just a second, as if she'd lost her train of thought. But surprises were her thing, so I knew she agreed, or at least she liked to be the one providing the surprise. She never let us know ahead of time what we'd be watching for Sunday night movie night. I liked it that way, as if I could tell Lauren's mood, how she was feeling, just from her movie choice.

"It's supposed to be entertaining," she continued. "It's from this guy called Giordano Pacino, and he's really hot."

"Hot like Liam Redwood?" I scrunched up my nose. Lauren finding the guy attractive did little to increase the movie's appeal.

She laughed. "I don't know what he looks like, but I meant hot like being talked about." She relaxed back into the pillows, then used her phone to switch off her bedroom light.

"I should warn you the reviews are saying it's scary." She used the TV remote to start the movie.

I snickered. I must have heard that warning a thousand times, but other than the occasional jump scare, which was no more than a cheap thrill, I was yet to find any of her movies scary.

The movie started with a heavy dose of atmosphere. The first shots were underwater, and it looked like they'd filmed it by putting a phone in a plastic bottle, submerging it and then pushing it around. There was nothing in the water so far, other than some fish shapes.

There were some nice lighting effects going on, which I figured were created by someone waving a flashlight around above the surface of the water. They did a commendable job with the eerie music and bubble sound effects, too.

"You think this is someone's bathtub?" I asked.

Lauren shushed me, but the corner of her mouth twitched up. She loved my comments. She would pretend she didn't and had even accused me of ruining movies by talking over them. But when she said it through laughter, I didn't believe her, and I had no intention of stopping.

A large shape glided through the water, like a dark shadow. Lauren tensed up beside me.

"Is this the scary part?" I asked.

"I don't think so. Not yet. This is just setting the scene."

But it wasn't just setting the scene. The rest of the movie continued the same way. Dark shapes moving through the water, the soundtrack speeding up to increase the tension before slowing down again, lulling us into a false sense of security, and then *bam!* The monster would rise out of the tub, giving us a brief glimpse before diving back down. The scares were predictable enough that Lauren didn't even flinch.

While I waited for something exciting to happen in the movie, I twisted some strands of Lauren's hair around my finger. She never objected when I played with her hair, and I liked to think she secretly enjoyed the attention. The first time I did it was well over a year ago. It had been an absentminded act, but Lauren didn't stop me, and I loved that she'd allowed it when she would've swatted other people away. So, the next time, it was deliberate. And now it was a habit.

On-screen, the monster took its latest victim, a woman with incredible legs—all we saw—and an impressive scream. As things progressed, they were showing us more and more of the monster, which was remarkably similar to someone in a wetsuit wearing an oversized green rubbery mask and covered in some matching goo. Unfortunately, the more we saw, the more it detracted from the terror of the unknown, and when the monster gurgled out its roar, I couldn't hold back my laugh.

"Shut up!" Lauren jabbed me with her elbow, but she was laughing too.

"I'm sorry." I straightened my face, trying to look deathly serious.

"That's better," Lauren said through her smile, before relaxing back down. We stayed in the same position, and I enjoyed every minute of our closeness, until the movie ended all too soon.

5

Jason

AS SOON AS the credits rolled, Lauren sat up, switched the light on with her phone, then turned to face me with an expectant expression. She always wanted to hear what I thought about whatever we watched before offering her own opinions.

"It was okay." I shrugged. "Suspenseful. The costumes weren't awful, but there wasn't much of a plot."

Lauren pursed her lips together. "So… that means you liked it?"

"Sure." I laughed. "You've made me watch worse."

She grinned. "Great, because I was hoping we could watch the sequel next time."

"There's a sequel already? I thought we were watching the festival nominees?"

"We are. They were both released this year, and both nominated. But it's the sequel that's getting the most buzz. Like I told you, Giordano Pacino is hot. So you'll watch it with me?"

"Of course I will."

Her grin widened, and I loved to see the excitement twinkling in her eyes, even if she was just fangirling over the director.

"How about Friday?" I suggested. "We could stay up late and have a double-feature?"

"You don't have a date on Friday?"

"No. Why would you think that?"

She reached for the remote control, switching off the TV, but it felt like she was trying to avoid looking at me. "I just thought you might, since I guess a lot of girls have been asking you out?" She made eye contact then, her brows raised in question.

I let out an annoyed sigh. We went over this at lunch yesterday, and talking about girls with Lauren was too awkward. She was the only one I wanted.

"So what?" I said. "Those girls are acting like I'm some kind of prize. It's not like they're actually interested. They don't even know me."

"They want to get to know you."

A low laugh escaped me as I shook my head. "I'm sure they'll get over it. It's like Emma said. They'll forget about me, and then things will go back to normal."

Lauren frowned, averting her gaze. Why was she questioning me about this?

It took a moment for me to catch on. I'd neglected our friendship while I was with Chloe, and Lauren must have thought I was going to do it again.

"Are you worried we won't get through the movie backlog?" I softened my voice. "I said I'd watch with you, and I will. I mean it, Lauren. The absolute last thing I want right now is a new girlfriend. Chloe was enough effort, and that wasn't even real."

Lauren laughed, but she still looked a little sad.

"So, Friday's okay with you?" I asked, and she nodded. "We'll watch two. The Beast from Beneath the Deep 2—"

"The Beast Babe from Beneath the Deep," Lauren corrected.

"Beast Babe? That sounds terrible."

"Not the best title, but it's supposed to be a lot like the first, just with more romance." Her lips twisted into a hopeful smile.

More romance? It could hardly have less.

"How could I say no to that?" I said. "So, we'll watch Beast Babe, and something else. Can you pick one that's funny? Intentionally funny?"

"I'll try."

We shared a moment of silence. This was the most time I'd spent alone with Lauren in months, and I was reluctant to leave so soon. But the movie was over, and I wasn't sure what else to say.

Plus, sitting so close always confused my brain over what was real and what was just fantasy. I wanted to pull her against me and kiss her senseless, but that wasn't something friends did. And since we were only friends, it was time to leave.

"I should get going." I pushed myself off the bed, then made my way over to the door.

Lauren jumped up, joining me by the door. But as I reached out to touch the handle, she leaned around me, putting her hand on top of mine. "Wait." She sounded almost panicked. "There's something I wanted to say."

31

I pulled my hand out from under hers, then twisted around to face her. "What's wrong?"

She was only inches away, frozen in place. She stared up at me, her mouth open, but silent.

I gazed down into her beautiful brown eyes, questioning her with mine. There was something wrong, but I was baffled as to what.

"Lauren? Talk to me?" I brushed her hair aside and placed my hand on her shoulder. I wanted to comfort her, but it didn't have the desired effect because she stepped back as if startled by my touch.

"I'm sorry. I was just being silly." She let out a nervous laugh.

"You're not silly. Tell me what's wrong?" My breath caught in my throat. I wasn't used to seeing Lauren like this.

"Nothing's wrong. I just wanted to tell you…" She paused, as if searching for the right words, "how happy I am to have you back."

She met my eyes again and gave me an embarrassed, lopsided smile. I laughed from the relief. She was only being sentimental, and even though that was unusual for Lauren, it was touching.

"Maybe you are a little silly," I said, and she responded by wrapping her arms around my chest, giving me a hug.

Her actions took me by complete surprise, so it was instinct that caused me to return the hug, pulling her tight against me.

"I missed you too, you know," I murmured into her hair.

In that moment, I was so tempted to tilt her head back and kiss her. It almost felt like I could get away with it, since we were already showing more emotion than usual. But I couldn't bring myself to do it. The fear of rejection was way too strong.

Lauren pulled away, looking bashful, and giving me a quick glance up through her thick lashes. "I'll walk you out."

She opened her bedroom door, and I followed her downstairs where I called out a goodbye to Keith and Tina, told Lauren I'd see her in the morning, then stepped out into the chilly December air.

What just happened in there? It was sweet that Lauren missed spending time with me, but she'd been acting beyond strange. I wished I knew why.

6

Lauren

I FLOPPED facedown onto my bed, then dragged my body over to where Jason had been sitting. It was still warm.

How had I messed up so badly? I'd made such a fool out of myself. As soon as I stopped him from opening the door, I knew I wouldn't be able to go through with it.

I pulled the pillow he'd been leaning against into my arms. It even smelled like him, fresh and woodsy, but that would fade fast, and soon it would be like he'd never been here at all.

Releasing the pillow, I grabbed for my phone instead. Emma made me promise to call her the instant Jason left. I didn't want to deal with her disappointment right now, but a promise was a promise, and it wasn't like the call would take long.

"Hello?" I could hear the anticipation in her voice.

"I couldn't do it."

"Oh, Lauren. What happened?"

"I stopped him when he was about to leave my room. But I couldn't get the words out, so instead I told him I was happy to have him back. And I already told him yesterday how much

I missed him. So now he probably thinks I was pining away the whole time. And then, to make things worse, I hugged him. He must think I'm nuts now, too."

Emma laughed. "I'm sure he's known that for years, and he doesn't seem to mind. But you've hugged Jason before. It's not that unusual."

"No. Not like this." A shiver ran down my spine as I remembered the way it felt when he held me close against him. "This was different."

"How so?"

"I don't know. It just felt maybe more intimate?"

The way he pulled me into him and told me he missed me too had sent tingles flying through my body. But I couldn't tell Emma what he said. She'd read too much into it. And I was already planning to dissect every little thing that had happened on my own.

"Well, that's good. It sounds like progress. But also like it might've been the perfect opportunity to share your feelings?"

"I know." I groaned. "But he'd literally just told me he didn't want a girlfriend. I mean, I know he doesn't feel the same, but—"

"You don't know that."

I clenched my jaw. If I thought Jason felt the same, it would be so easy to tell him. But Emma was living in a fantasy world where all it took was me confessing my feelings before we rode into the sunset. Real life wasn't like that.

We'd been over all the arguments so many times, and ever since Sunday's revelations, almost every conversation had been about Jason. I didn't want to go over everything again.

"Even if he doesn't feel the same, you should still tell him," Emma continued. She'd said all this before. That it would be worth confessing, just to stop torturing myself. To stop myself from obsessing and to get some closure.

Jason would be nice about it. He'd let me down gently. But just imagining the pity in his eyes made me nauseous. How could I deliberately set myself up for rejection?

That was tough, and it was why I failed tonight.

"I know," I said. "I'm still planning to tell him."

"You are? Really?"

"I think so. When the moment's right."

It was Emma's turn to groan.

"Let's not talk about Jason anymore." I forced my voice to sound determined. "I mean at all. We're just going in circles. I know what I have to do. Talking about it won't make that happen."

"Okay. What do you want to talk about instead?"

I paused. There was still only one thing on my mind, but there was a topic that always got Emma excited. "How are things with Kai?"

That set her going. Even though she wasn't comfortable sharing the more intimate details, she would happily talk about Kai for hours. I didn't mind listening, but all I could think of was how much I wanted what she and Kai had, and how it would be up to me to make it happen.

7

Jason

BY WEDNESDAY, things were noticeably better at school. The attention from the past couple of days was easing off. And while flattering, the interest in me had only been surface deep. It wasn't what I wanted.

"Jason!" Chloe called out from down the hallway before running up to me.

We'd spent so much time together over the past few months that this week had been a stark contrast. Her relationship with Nate was still brand new though, so I was trying to give them space.

But we hadn't had a conversation since Monday when she'd called me over to her table at lunch, something she'd apparently only done so that she could tell everyone how wonderful I was. She'd gone way overboard with the praise.

"Hey there." I gave her a smile. "How are things going?"

"Incredible. I still can't believe how nice everyone is being. Honestly, I feel kind of stupid now. The lengths we went to hiding the truth. And that I made you go along with it... I'm so sorry."

37

"Don't worry about it. I'm glad things are going well. And you and Nate look good together."

She grinned. "He's amazing. But anyway, I want to make it up to you."

"You've done enough." I laughed. "You wouldn't believe how many girls have asked me out this week. And it's all because of what you've been telling them. Lies and more lies."

"It's all true, I·swear. But seriously, I want to help you. Like you helped me."

"Help me with what?"

"Your love life, of course."

"You think I need help?" I didn't know whether to laugh or be offended.

"Yes, and it's already working."

I shook my head. "Thanks, Chloe, but I don't want any help. Besides, I think most of those girls have already lost interest."

"I'm not trying to help you with those girls. Unless you want me to? I was trying to help you with Lauren."

"With Lauren?"

"Yes. And like I said, it's already working. We're making her so jealous. It's written all over her face."

I stared at Chloe in disbelief.

"Don't look at me like that. I know it wasn't the main reason you agreed to help me, but isn't this what you wanted? To make her jealous?"

Even though that was true, I shook my head. Chloe knew I'd hoped to make someone jealous, but I'd never admitted who, and I didn't intend to share my feelings now. "Look, Chloe. I know you have good intentions, but I've told you before, Lauren doesn't see me like that. If she was acting jealous, it's only because I promised to watch some terrible monster movies with her, and she was worried if I got a new girlfriend that I'd disappear on her again. But we already talked it through, and I reassured her, so we're cool."

Chloe frowned. "Okay. I'll try not to interfere too much. But if you change your mind, I'm here for you. I'll do whatever I can to help. I mean it. Just let me know."

I nodded. Her heart was in the right place, but Chloe needed to back off.

With a warm smile, Chloe turned away from me. Then she whipped back around. "I almost forgot to tell you. Mia wants to throw me a party."

Mia was one of Chloe's best friends. She lived in a huge house, and from what Chloe told me, her parents were out of town way more often than they were home.

The freedom Mia had was unbelievable. Even though Mom was relaxed about giving me independence, I couldn't imagine her wanting to leave me home alone for days, let alone weeks.

I'd gone to a few of Mia's parties over the past few months, and they were fun. But one for Chloe? I searched my brain, trying to recall any mention of her birthday, but I drew a blank.

"It'll be a casual get-together, keeping it small this time."

"It's for you?"

"Yes. She says it's to celebrate having me back."

That made sense. Chloe had distanced herself from her friends, avoiding activities that might have given away her family situation. They must have missed her. Plus, I was certain Mia loved hosting and would take any opportunity to have friends over.

"Sounds fun. When is it?"

"Friday."

I sucked in a breath. "Sorry. I already have plans with Lauren on Friday."

"A date?" Her eyes widened.

"Of course not. We're just getting together to watch some movies."

"*Terrible* movies?"

"Yeah, those." I laughed. "But I promised, so I don't want to cancel on her."

"You can watch movies any time, but the party has to be on Friday because Mia's brother, Josh, is coming home soon for winter break, and she doesn't want him to be there. Please, Jason, you have to come. And Lauren too. I'm sure she won't want to miss it."

Chloe was probably right, and if Lauren would prefer to go to the party, then that was what we'd do. The Beast Babe could wait.

"I'll talk to her about it."

"Great. I'll see you two on Friday then." She gave me a confident grin before sauntering away.

With Chloe gone, I pulled out my phone and typed out a message to Lauren. Either way, I'd get to spend Friday evening with her, but I couldn't stop myself from hoping she'd want to stick to the original plan, and that we would spend it alone.

8

Lauren

"EVERY ROOM HAS A DIFFERENT THEME, so if we want to reserve specific ones, we'll need to book early."

I nodded in agreement. I'd already promised to check out the website of the quirky hotel Emma had found, but she'd been talking about it non-stop since we got out of our last class. Her big blue eyes brimmed with excitement, and although I couldn't contribute much to the discussion, I was enjoying her enthusiasm.

Operation not-talking-about-Jason had been a success so far, and instead we focused on planning our road trip. The possibilities were endless, and we still hadn't even decided on a route. If we went to all the fun places Emma had discovered, our trip would need to take a year.

"I'm torn between the medieval room or the neon dystopia. They're both so different, but—"

Emma's phone buzzed from within her backpack.

"That'll be Kai. I sent him the links earlier to see which he preferred."

Emma retrieved her phone and her expression lifted even higher as she read her long message.

"Well? Which does he like best?" I asked.

"Oh, that wasn't Kai. It was Chloe. She said Mia's having a party on Friday, and we all have to go."

"On Friday? I can't. I have plans with—with you know who."

"You can say his name, Lauren. He's not the Dark Lord. But Chloe says she just talked to Jason, and he wants to go."

"He does?" My heart sank. I'd been looking forward to watching movies all night on Friday and had even talked myself into having a second attempt at confessing my feelings.

"That's what Chloe said. Don't look so sad. You can reschedule your movies, and you'll see Jason at the party. Chloe says there won't be many people, so you'll still be together all night."

"I guess." It was true I spent most of my time at Mia's previous parties with Jason, even though he'd supposedly been dating Chloe at the time.

My phone beeped from my pocket.

JASON

> Did you hear about Mia's party? Want to go? I'm happy either way

Flipping my phone, I showed Emma the message. "It doesn't sound like he's decided."

"So it's up to you. But if it makes any difference, I want you to come to the party."

I nodded, but the school bell cut our conversation short. We'd talk about it again later.

BY THE END of the day, Jason and I had agreed to reschedule our movie double-feature and go to the party instead. He was relaxed about both options, but Emma and Chloe were both piling on the pressure, so it would've been a fight to say no.

"I'm so excited. You won't regret this," Emma said while we waited next to Jason's car after school.

"Why are you so excited? It's just a small party." She was almost too eager, and that made me anxious.

She paused, as if having an internal debate about whether to confide in me.

"It's because I have an idea to help you," she admitted, before biting her lip in a nervous smile. "Do you remember when we played truth or dare that time at Mia's?"

"Do I remember?" I gawked at her. Nate had dared Emma to kiss Kai. It was their first kiss together, and it had been smoking hot. I didn't think anyone there that night would ever be able to wipe the image from their memories.

Emma blushed. "Well, we thought that if we played again—"

"No." I held up my hands to cut her off. "If I kiss Jason, I want it to be because he wants to, not because of a dare, and absolutely not in front of an audience."

Emma scowled, and I could understand why. I was a giant hypocrite. I'd encouraged her to get more physical with Kai. But it had been different between them, because it had been obvious they liked each other.

"Actually, that wasn't what I was going to say."

KENZIE BRAYNE

"It wasn't? What's your idea then?"

"We were thinking—"

"What do you mean, we?" I interrupted her again. "Did you tell Kai?"

Emma winced, and my mouth dropped open in horror. I trusted Emma. She wouldn't share my secret, would she?

"I didn't tell him directly, but he was there when Nate was asking questions—"

"Nate was asking questions?" My jaw dropped even lower.

She nodded. "I swear I didn't tell them anything, but they kind of guessed."

I covered my face with my hands in humiliation. Kai and Nate knew how I felt about Jason, and Nate probably told Chloe, which would explain her comments on Monday. This was horrible. How would I be able to face any of them now?

"Does everyone know? Nate must have told Chloe, right?" I asked, still hiding.

"Oh, that's the best part! Chloe already thought Jason liked you."

My breath caught. "Are you serious?" I moved my hands away from my face and grabbed hold of Emma's arms. "Did he say something to her?"

"Well, no, I don't think so. But it doesn't mean it's not true."

I dropped her arms and sighed. Why did I let myself get my hopes up so easily?

"So, will you let us do my plan? If you don't give permission, I'll tell Chloe no. But trust us, please. I think you'll love it." There was pleading in her eyes.

I sighed again. "Tell me the plan."

Emma shook her head. "I don't want to ruin it. But come

on, Lauren, say yes. It's the least you can do after lying to me about the bet."

I frowned. I'd told a little white lie to help Emma get together with Kai. I'd considered it a helping hand, but Emma might have preferred the word interference. She was mad when she found out, but ultimately my plan worked, and she forgave me long ago. But she wasn't letting me forget.

"You won't dare me to kiss Jason? Or force me to admit anything?"

Emma shook her head, and the smile was spreading over her face. She knew I was about to give in.

"Fine," I said with a slight scowl, even though I'd probably regret it. "But I'm trusting you, Emma. You know my limits."

She grinned. "This is going to be amazing. I'm so excited for you."

It was crazy to agree to Emma's plan, but I was running out of options. I'd tried to tell Jason how I felt, and failed. And even before I embarrassed myself last night, I'd been waiting forever for the right moment that never came. It was time to accept that I couldn't do it on my own.

I needed to be pushed.

9

Jason

EMMA WAS ACTING strange on the way home from school. She had a huge grin plastered across her face and seemed overly excited about the party on Friday.

She was clutching her phone in her hand, and messages were flying back and forth between her and Chloe.

"Chloe says we should all get ready together again," Emma said to Lauren.

"Yeah, okay. But isn't it a casual thing? I don't want to get dressed up."

"Yes, it's casual. But it's still fun to get ready together. We should do it at your house this time." Emma didn't give Lauren a chance to object before continuing. "And since we'll already be together, we should ride together too. Kai says he can pick us up around eight, and then we'll get you on the way too, Jason."

"I don't need a ride, thanks," I said. "I'm not planning to drink, so I can drive myself."

"No, come with us. It'll be more fun. Plus, it's more environmentally friendly."

Lauren laughed, and I glanced over, our eyes meeting. She gave a small shrug.

"Okay, if you insist," I answered Emma.

"Perfect. I'll let him know." She returned her attention to her phone.

"You're texting Kai?" Lauren asked. "I thought it was Chloe?"

"Chloe and Kai, well, Kai's sister since he's driving. Oh, and Mia."

Lauren twisted around to shoot Emma a look.

"I just wanted to get the plans cemented while we're together." Emma sounded defensive. "And we're all set now, so feel free to talk about something else."

Turning back, Lauren shared a bemused look with me. But neither of us said anything, leaving it to Emma to change the subject.

"Did Lauren tell you about the hotel I found?"

"No. What hotel?"

"It's this amazing place where all the rooms have different themes and you can choose which you want. I've narrowed it down to two, but Kai likes the neon dystopia room, so I expect we'll go for that. It has this whole cyberpunk vibe going on and looks incredible. You guys should totally get the medieval one, which is my second choice. And if it turns out to be better, maybe we can swap." She chuckled.

I laughed with her to be polite, but I couldn't stop myself from tensing up, my fingers gripping harder onto the steering wheel. Emma was assuming Lauren and I would share a room? It made sense financially, but we hadn't discussed it.

I hadn't slept in the same room as Lauren for years, and even then, we'd been in a group. This would be just the two of us, alone, and although Emma hadn't mentioned it, I figured those kinds of rooms would only have one bed.

And the idea of sharing a bed with Lauren made my heart hammer. I stared ahead at the road, waiting to see if she said anything in response to Emma's comment, but she stayed silent.

"You'll have to send me the link," I said.

"I'll do it now." Emma returned her attention to her phone, and a few seconds later, mine beeped with the new message. "But we really need to get together as a group, sort out our route, make plans. There are so many places I want to go, but I know it's not only up to me. How about this time next week? Wednesday, maybe after dinner? You can all come to my house. My parents will be out, which is perfect since I keep forgetting to tell them Kai's coming on the road trip."

Lauren laughed. Emma always acted like her parents were overprotective, even though I wasn't sure it was true. The idea of a co-ed road trip wouldn't thrill her dad, but I didn't think he'd try to forbid it. Besides, we'd all be eighteen by then.

"Wednesday sounds good to me," I said.

The only thing I had planned next week was the double-feature with Lauren, which we'd pushed back until Monday. I secretly hoped we'd be able to get in another movie night or two next week, but we could arrange those one at a time. I wouldn't mention it until leaving her house on Monday. I didn't want to appear too eager.

AS SOON AS I parked my car in the driveway, I reached for my phone. I hadn't been able to get the thought of sharing a bed with Lauren out of my head for the rest of the drive home, and my imagination had been running wild.

Emma had sent me two links, so I tapped on the first, opening up the webpage for the neon room. Emma was right that it looked incredible; they hadn't scrimped on the theming. But one feature drew my eye—the singular gigantic bed in the center of the room. I opened up the second link, and it too only had one bed.

I blew out a long breath, trying to slow my breathing. Why was I freaking out about this now? The road trip was six months away, and a lot could change in that time. Hopefully it would.

After unbuckling my seatbelt, I climbed out of the car. My distracted mind was only now registering the scene on the other side of the street. The house opposite had been empty for months, but now there was a moving truck outside.

If the exterior of the property reflected the interior, it would need a lot of fixing up. I hoped the new owners were up to the challenge.

The movers were carrying boxes inside one at a time, and there was a young woman with cropped black hair standing in the front yard, holding a child in each arm. I wasn't good at guessing children's ages, but these two appeared the same, probably twins. They must have been heavy to carry at the same time, but they looked as if they'd crawl away and get into trouble if she put them on the floor, so holding them was likely a necessity.

No wonder the woman looked so tired. Moving was bad enough as it was. From across the street, she caught my eye. I gave a friendly wave, but of course she couldn't return it and instead nodded hello. I jogged over to greet her, and as I got closer I noticed that she only had one arm inside her padded red coat, and that on the other side, underneath one of her kids, her arm was in a cast.

"Hi, I'm Jason. I live across the street." I pointed to my house. "Welcome to Sunset Vista Street."

"Thanks. It's good to meet you, Jason. I'm Marina, and this is Tommy"—she tilted her head to the left and then to the right—"and Alex."

"Twins?"

She nodded. "They're the reason we moved. I'm a freelance writer, so I can work from anywhere, and I thought Haven Valley sounded like the perfect place to create a peaceful home for the boys. The change of scenery is refreshing, and I can't wait to see all the awe-inspiring sunsets."

I smiled. "Don't let the optimistic street name fool you, but there are some incredible views from Haven Hill."

"Thanks for the tip. I can't wait to explore the area as soon as we're settled."

"Where are you from?"

"Most recently, LA." Marina looked down at Tommy balanced on her cast. "Is it just you and your parents across the street? Any siblings?"

"It's only me and my mom. She's working nights at the moment, otherwise I'm sure she'd be right over with a welcome pie or something."

I glanced back at my house as I spoke. Mom's car was there, but she was probably sleeping. Her nursing shifts at the hospital could be erratic, and I was never sure when she'd be at home, and awake.

Marina smiled. "It's just the three of us too."

I wasn't about to ask where the twins' father was, but it had to be tough being on her own. Studying her face, I decided Marina couldn't be more than a few years older than me. She had attractive features, but the exhaustion had taken its toll.

One of the movers called over at her. "Where do you want these?"

"Everything marked with a star in the garage, please."

She turned back to me. "It's total chaos. We've been unloading for the past two hours. I'm telling them where to put stuff but have lost the list of what's what. And with my broken arm, I'm about as useful as a chocolate teapot." She let out a tired laugh.

I cringed in sympathy. "Is there anything I can do to help?"

"Unless you have x-ray vision and can tell me what's in the boxes, I don't think so. But thank you."

"No problem. But if there's anything I can do once you're settled in, just give me a shout. I know how to work a paint-brush." I moved my arm up and down, demonstrating an impressively fluid painting motion.

She laughed. "Well, since you're offering, I'm getting a delivery of furniture on Friday. The kind that needs to be assembled. I was planning to construct it on my own, but I'm not sure how well I'll manage until the cast is off, so an extra pair of hands might be a good idea. I'll pay you, of course."

"I'd be happy to help, and you can pay me in snacks while we work."

"That would be amazing. I'd truly appreciate any help, even if it's only in deciphering the instructions." She smiled again, and it took years off her. "So, would you be able to come over after school on Friday? You're still in high school, aren't you?"

"Yeah, I'm a senior. I kind of already have plans for Friday, but I could help on Saturday, if that works?"

"That absolutely works. Thank you so much. Come over whenever you have time. I'll be here all day, unpacking."

I nodded, then said goodbye to Marina before crossing back over to my house.

In the kitchen, I tossed my backpack onto the table. I'd stay down here so as not to disturb Mom, but hopefully we'd have a chance to talk later.

I hadn't spoken to her face to face for days, and I still needed to tell her the truth about Chloe.

10

Jason

"GOOD MORNING." Mom's voice rang out close behind me about an hour later. She was stealthy and had somehow sneaked up without me noticing.

Leaning over, she gave me a kiss on my temple before virtually skipping to the coffee machine.

She was wearing her fluffy white robe and was acting surprisingly chipper for someone about to go to work.

I closed my textbook. I'd been engrossed in a math problem, but now I'd lost my train of thought, and instead the nerves were kicking in.

"What's wrong?" Mom asked.

My mouth dropped open. Mom was occupied making her coffee, which I wasn't convinced she needed. She couldn't have done more than glance at me, yet somehow she knew something was wrong?

Mom had reacted with suspicion when I told her I was dating Chloe. She'd fired questions at me, and I lied my socks off. I hated every fabrication, but I didn't feel as guilty as I expected, thanks to Mom's uncanny ability to see right through me. It was as if she knew I wasn't interested in Chloe, and even worse, she knew why.

She'd pursed her lips and stared, before brushing off my relationship as some kind of phase. Like I just wanted to play the field before getting serious with Lauren, because yes, Mom was another person who was expecting us to get together. And even though she'd been supportive, she hadn't hidden her reservations about me dating Chloe.

I cleared my throat. "I have something to tell you."

Mom turned to face me, her forehead wrinkled with concern.

"It's not bad," I added, and Mom's features softened.

"Let me get my coffee. Have you finished your homework?"

"Almost. I can get it finished tonight."

It wouldn't take me long to get done once she left for work and I was home alone again. I wished I'd suggested another movie night with Lauren, but I hadn't wanted to appear too desperate to spend time with her. It was stupid though. She was every bit as enthusiastic about having more movie nights, albeit for a different reason than me.

Mom poured her coffee while I waited. Then she pulled out a chair, joining me at the small kitchen table. She cradled the mug in her hands and took a sip before fixing her attention on me, raising her eyebrows in expectation.

"It's about me and Chloe."

Mom didn't react at all, so I continued, deciding it was better to tell the story step-by-step so she could understand, rather than blurting out the truth like I was tempted to do.

"You remember how I said we hit it off in the park where I went running?"

Mom nodded, but the confusion was back on her face, so I told her the story, letting the details flood out. How I'd offered Chloe a ride home when a sudden storm had hit. How she cried and admitted the house I took her to was no longer her home. How afraid she was of people finding out. And how I'd offered to drive her to school, so that she wouldn't have to take the bus or tell her friends she was living with her grandparents in a far less affluent neighborhood.

A scowl grew on Mom's face while she listened to me talk, but she didn't interrupt. I explained that we'd agreed the rides to school would only look believable if we were dating, but I missed out one small detail. How, thanks to a book Chloe was reading, I'd come up with a laughable idea—that having a girlfriend might help Lauren see me in a new light. That it might make her jealous.

"So, we decided to pretend to date, to fake a relationship. It was only supposed to be for a few weeks. Chloe thought things would get better at home, but they didn't." I clenched my jaw and swallowed as I waited for Mom's reaction. She wouldn't flip out, but I feared seeing disappointment in her eyes. "I'm sorry for lying to you."

"Oh, Jason." Mom shook her head in disbelief. "You need to learn to say no."

That was what she got from my story? That I was a pushover? But it hadn't been like that.

"I wanted to help her, Mom."

"Of course you did. You always want to help everyone." She frowned at me, as if that were a bad thing, even though it was a trait I'd inherited from her. "I'm guessing things are over now. That's why you're telling me?"

I nodded. "Everyone knows, and no one even cares. Chloe

had been so desperate to hide the truth, but..." I let out a small laugh as I shrugged.

Mom took a long sip of her coffee. "What does Lauren think of all this?"

I shrugged again, realizing I didn't know the answer to her question. Lauren had reacted with shock to the revelations, and while plenty of other girls showed me what they thought of my actions, Lauren hadn't told me anything. I had no idea whether she agreed I was some kind of knight in shining armor, or more likely a schmuck for going along with it. But either way, I knew one thing.

"She's glad it's over. She said she missed me."

"I'm sure she did."

I tried not to react to the implication in Mom's tone.

"I guess it'll be my turn to miss you the most now? If you'll be spending every waking minute making up lost time with Lauren?"

I laughed. "Not quite every minute, although I'm going over to watch movies on Monday night. Oh, and there's a party on Friday, but I'll be here the rest of the time, unless I'm at school. Not that it's fair to guilt trip me, Mom, I can't keep up with your shifts."

She sighed. "Neither can I. In fact, I'd better get ready now. But I have Saturday off, so we should do something fun together. We still need to pick out our Christmas tree."

I nodded, even though Mom's sleep cycles were all over the place and she might not be awake much during the day. Then I remembered.

"I can't. I promised our new neighbor I'd help build some furniture on Saturday."

"Our new neighbor? Someone moved in?" Mom perked up with interest.

"Yeah, her name's Marina and she has some little kids. Twins. She seemed nice, but exhausted."

"And you offered to help her build furniture?"

"Yeah. She has a broken arm. Plus she's a single mom." I didn't need to explain further. Mom understood what I was saying. Even though I'd been too young to remember it well, I knew Mom struggled when I was younger.

"I'll look forward to meeting her." Mom gave me a smile as she stood. "Maybe I can help with the construction efforts?"

I grimaced, making her laugh as she ruffled her hand through my hair. It was best Mom stayed away if Marina wanted her furniture to stand up on its own.

She gave me another kiss, this time on the top of my head, before heading back upstairs. I smiled to myself as I returned to my math homework. Mom took my confession better than I'd expected, and now everyone knew the truth.

The fuss was dying down at school, and other than my new friendship with Chloe, nothing had changed.

Life was almost back to normal.

11

Lauren

DAD WAS TEASING Chloe about her relationship with Jason, and it was painful. He'd joked with Emma about her having a fake boyfriend too, but Emma had heard it all before and was used to him. Chloe, however, had only met Dad once before in passing, so his comments were too much.

"Let's go upstairs." I linked arms with Chloe, who, for some inexplicable reason, was laughing at Dad's jokes. Didn't she realize she was only encouraging him?

"Don't leave yet, girls. We need to make plans." Dad forced his face to look serious. I rolled my eyes, having seen this facial expression a thousand times before. Emma also knew he was setting up a joke, and she reacted with a grin.

"Later, Dad, we need to get ready." I tugged on Chloe's arm.

But she didn't budge and instead fell right into his trap. "Plans for what?"

"For Lauren here." He tilted his head as he inspected me. "Isn't it about time we found a fake boyfriend for you too?"

I glowered back at him while Chloe laughed again.

Dad exaggerated an expression of terror. "Maybe not."

This time, when I pulled on Chloe's arm, she allowed me to guide her over to the stairs, leaving Emma trailing behind carrying their bags, which were both unnecessarily large.

"I'm so sorry about him," I said once we were safe in my room. "He thinks he's hilarious."

"And you don't find him funny?" Chloe arched a perfectly manicured brow.

Normally I did, but tonight I was too anxious. I must have been out of my mind when I agreed to go along with Emma's little scheme. I'd tried to back out of it, but that only made her more determined. She'd reiterated that I needed to trust her and reminded me why I needed her help. And she was right. I trusted her, and I needed her help, even if I wasn't entirely convinced I wanted it.

Chloe was looking at me, waiting for an answer, but Emma stepped in. "She's just excited about tonight."

Chloe nodded but didn't ask any questions. Even if she knew how I felt about Jason, the last thing I wanted was to be forced to discuss my feelings out loud.

"So, have you chosen what to wear?" Chloe asked.

I waved my hand down my body.

Chloe's eyes followed my hand's journey, then she looked back at my face and blinked. "Are you serious?"

I pushed my lips to the side and nodded. I'd been told tonight was casual, so jeans and a plain gray t-shirt it was.

Chloe sighed. "What about your hair and makeup?"

"Chloe, she looks great already." Emma hugged her arm around my shoulders in a united front.

"Sure, but it's fun to do a little something extra, to add

emphasis and make your features pop. How about just eye makeup or some lip gloss?"

"Okay," I answered. "I don't mind some lip gloss. But that's all."

If I was trying to get Jason's attention anywhere on my body, my mouth seemed a good option. My heart fluttered at the thought of him noticing, staring at my lips, as if he might want to kiss them.

I shook away the thought. That wouldn't happen. Jason hadn't ever looked at me in that way, and lip gloss was unlikely to change anything.

Chloe grinned in response. "Great. We'll do that before we leave. But first, is there somewhere I can change?" She picked her bag up off the floor where Emma had dumped it.

"The bathroom is the second door on the left," I said.

"Thanks. Can you show me?"

I glanced over at Emma, expecting to share the amusement of Chloe requesting a chaperone, but she was busy rummaging in her bag.

"Um, okay." I pulled my bedroom door open, then walked with Chloe down to the bathroom and opened the door for her. "Here it is."

"Thanks. While you're here, could you help me with my top?"

Holding her oversized gym bag with one hand, Chloe began searching through with the other.

"Did you pack enough?" I held back a snicker. I was used to Chloe bringing excessive amounts of makeup with her the few times we'd gotten ready together at Emma's house, but this was overkill.

"I like to be prepared, and I wanted to get your opinion on

which top to wear, so I brought a couple. They're from a few seasons ago, but I don't think anyone will notice."

She wanted my opinion? Even though I knew nothing about fashion?

"Here's one." She pulled out a scrap of fabric. It was black with a shimmery silver thread running through it. "Hold it for me?" She shoved it into my hand then returned to rooting through her bag. "I know there's another one in here somewhere."

I held up the top she'd handed me, and it glimmered under the bathroom lights. This was something you'd wear to a club, not to a casual hang out in a friend's basement. It was both low cut and cropped, so it barely covered anything.

"Can you hold these too, please?" Chloe didn't wait for an answer before thrusting some makeup palettes at me. I cradled my arms together to prevent myself from dropping them. Then she added more clothing and accessories to the pile, piece by piece, until there was far more in my arms than remaining in her bag.

"Are you sure you packed it?" I asked.

"Yes, it's definitely here somewhere." She paused before laughing. "I'm sorry. I forgot I stuffed it in the side pocket."

She unzipped the pocket and pulled out a deep red top, before adding it to my hand, which was still clasping the first top.

"The rest can go back in my bag," she said, before starting the process in reverse, taking items off me one at a time and neatly putting them away.

Once finished, she took the two tops from me, giving me her bag to hold instead.

"Well?" She held them both up. "Which do you think Nate would like more?"

After observing Nate and Chloe at school together all week, I was confident he would drool over her even if she were wearing a garbage bag. But he was still a guy, so the answer seemed obvious.

"The sexy one." I fixed my eyes on the black top. Chloe would look incredible wearing that, mostly because she had the confidence to pull it off.

Chloe nodded in agreement, but then she wavered. "You don't like the red one? I think it's kind of sexy too." She pulled at the fabric in the air so I could see the style. It was fairly simple, but the neckline was still dangerously low.

"I'm sure Nate would love that too," I answered. "The red one is more casual though, so maybe save the black top for one of Mia's make-an-effort parties."

"I guess. I was just thinking if I wear the black top maybe you'd want to borrow the red one?"

I shook my head adamantly. We'd already established I was wearing a t-shirt, and I wasn't about to change my mind. Although now I was wondering how Jason might react if I turned up in something so revealing. Would he even look twice?

Chloe might have attempted to persuade me, but a knock on the door interrupted us.

"What's going on in there? You guys are taking forever," Emma called from the other side.

Leaving Chloe alone to get changed, I joined Emma outside the bathroom. "Sorry. She couldn't find the top she wanted to wear."

Emma didn't seem interested in the explanation, though, and she hurried me back into my bedroom.

"How are you feeling?" she asked as I climbed onto my bed.

"I'm still not sure this is a good idea. I wish you would tell me what you're planning."

"But you're still going to go ahead with it, right? You're ready to tell Jason how you feel about him? Tonight?"

I exhaled, unsure if I'd ever be ready. But I was going crazy. I needed to confess, to find out if I had a chance. So I nodded, making Emma squeal in excitement and join me on the bed for a hug.

"Am I interrupting something?" Chloe asked from the doorway with an amused smile. She'd changed into the red top.

"No." Emma released me. "We're just excited about tonight. And we need to finish getting ready. Kai will be here soon."

Chloe sprang into action. She sat Emma down at my desk and effortlessly transformed her into a goddess with only a light application of makeup. I would need a truckload to look that good, if it were even possible.

Whenever I attempted to apply makeup, I ended up looking like a clown. And the thought of letting Chloe work on me with her incredible skills and still not getting results was enough to prevent me from letting her even try.

After she was done with Emma, Chloe worked on her own makeup. Meanwhile, I got up off the bed, and armed with my favorite hairbrush, I brushed my hair, which I was leaving down tonight. Emma was going for a similar style, leaving her long blonde hair flowing over her shoulders.

Chloe caught my eye in her mirror. "I wish I had your hair."

"You do?"

I was used to getting compliments on my hair, and I knew other people considered it my best feature, even though it sometimes annoyed the hell out of me. Truth be told, and as sad as it might be, if I hadn't thought Jason liked it, I probably would have lopped it off years ago. But that Chloe could be at all envious of me was staggering.

"Yeah. You can just fall out of bed, run a brush through and look perfect. If I want any kind of volume, I need products followed by more products and even then my hair will be flat by the end of the day."

My jaw dropped, and I was about to answer back, but the sound of the doorbell downstairs stopped me.

Emma jumped up right away. "That'll be Kai. I need to go save him from your dad." She picked up her bag, lugging it with her as she left as quickly as she could manage.

Emma was right to be concerned. Dad was in one of those extra playful moods tonight, and he would no doubt extend his teasing to Kai too, even though they'd only met a handful of times.

"Let's hurry up." I chucked my hairbrush down onto my bed.

"Okay, okay." Chloe prodded at herself one last time with a makeup brush before she started packing everything away into her bag. "Wait. We forgot your lip gloss."

"Don't worry about it."

"It'll only take five seconds." She turned to me, wielding the lip gloss wand in her hand like a weapon. "Now stand still."

Impatient to get downstairs, I let Chloe have her way, leaving my lips feeling silky, without the tacky sensation I'd expected.

"You look very kissable," she said with a teasing lilt to her voice.

How was I supposed to react to that? Did she really believe the plan would work, and I'd get to kiss Jason tonight?

Chloe scooped her bag up with one arm, and before I responded to her comment or even glanced in the mirror, she guided me downstairs, where Emma was waiting for us.

"I sent Kai back to the car," she told us in a hushed voice. "Let's go before your dad sees Chloe and starts with the jokes again."

I nodded. Sneaking out wasn't necessary, but for Chloe's sake, it was probably safest.

And it was no effort. No one tried to stop us as we left the house and met Kai at his car. Emma sat in the front, her reward for being the only one able to open the passenger door which always stuck.

As we drove the short distance to Jason's house, I questioned my sanity. Who in their right mind would agree to go along with a plan when they didn't know what it was? I debated with myself until the point that Jason joined us, looking as incredible as ever in a casual yellow t-shirt. I shifted over to the middle and he slid in next to me, greeting us all with his friendly smile as his leg bumped against my knee.

That was when the panic set in and I knew. No matter how much Emma tried to persuade me, I had to do this on my own terms. I needed to stop whatever she was planning.

Before it was too late.

12

Jason

WE'D ONLY BEEN in Mia's basement for about ten minutes, but already it felt like something was off. Emma was acting highly excitable, and Kai had to keep pulling her against his body to stop her from bouncing off the walls.

Lauren was the opposite. As soon as we came downstairs after grabbing drinks in the high-end kitchen, she'd claimed a seat on the couch, which she was now sharing with Chloe and Nate. Despite trying, they weren't quite managing to include her in their conversation, and instead, she kept glancing over at Emma with a mild look of apprehension.

What was going on?

The whole setup tonight was different from when I'd been here before. For the other parties, Mia had decorated the base-ment and added some blow-up furniture. But now, with only the couch and the dance floor in the corner as permanent fixtures, the large room felt empty.

Especially since we were such a small crowd. I was cool with it though. Happy just to chill for the night, even though

I'd prefer to be alone with Lauren watching her monster movies.

The only other people here were Mia and her best friend, Allie. Both girls were petite, but while Mia was slim with dark hair, Allie was blonde with an hourglass figure.

"We honestly thought you were a little controlling," Allie told me. "Because of how Chloe always had to check with you before she could go anywhere."

I nodded in understanding. Chloe needed to ask because she was relying on me to drive her around.

"And then once she told us the truth, everything started making sense. You helped her so much, and I know she wants to make it up to you. You're her hero. And if Chloe didn't made me promise, I would totally have been first in line—"

"Allie!" Mia interrupted her, looping her arm over her friend's shoulders, then turning to me. "What she means is that now we know what was actually going on, we want to get to know you better."

"Exactly." Allie beamed a dazzling smile in my direction. "And I know the best way to get to know someone. We should play."

"Play what?" Emma asked as she and Kai joined us.

"Truth or dare," Allie answered with a grin, and Emma bobbed her head in enthusiastic agreement.

"I'm game," Kai said. "I enjoyed the last time I played." He leaned over to give Emma a quick kiss on her cheek.

"So did I." She smiled up at him, and just like that, without asking the rest of us, they'd decided.

"Come on, guys," Allie called over to our friends on the couch. "It's truth or dare time. Everyone make a circle on the floor."

Chloe jumped up from her seat, then pulling Nate with her, she moved over to the floor where the circle was already forming.

Lauren didn't move a muscle. "I'll sit this one out."

Not wanting to miss my opportunity, I joined her on the couch. "Yeah, me too."

"What? No!" Emma frowned. "You guys have to play."

Lauren shook her head. "No really, Em. I'll pass."

But Emma didn't want to listen. Instead, she reached for Lauren's hand and yanked her up. "Come on, you know it'll be worth it. Trust me." Then she turned to me with a pleading expression.

If Lauren was playing, I would too, so I moved to sit in the space between Kai and Mia.

"This is always fun with new couples," Allie said. "It's a great way to find out how comfortable you are with each other." She wiggled her eyebrows, and Chloe groaned, even though when I glanced at her she was grinning.

"No recordings allowed, so I want everyone's phones out of the way." Allie demonstrated by pushing her phone out of arm's reach behind her, and we all dutifully did the same. "Great. I'll kick things off. Nate, truth or dare?

Nate reclined on his hands as a confident smirk spread over his face. "Dare."

Allie smiled. "This is just to set the tone, not because I actually want to see it. But I dare you to make out with Chloe's ear."

"What?" Chloe's eyebrows shot up and she laughed. "Is that even possible?"

"Just lick it then," Allie said.

Nate pulled Chloe closer toward him. "We haven't even done this in private yet, but sure."

"Yet?" Chloe grimaced, but she didn't complain as Nate leaned in. He whispered something—only for her—before sticking out his tongue and making contact with the top of her ear.

Chloe held still, keeping her face neutral as Nate trailed his tongue down to her earlobe. He moved with precision, then reversed the action, blowing out a steady breath over her skin.

I glanced at Lauren. She was staring, much like everyone else was, at the spectacle in front of us.

Nate ran his tongue back down Chloe's ear. He sucked her lobe, possibly nibbling, before releasing it and ending with a gentle kiss on her cheek. Chloe couldn't hide her smile.

That was one of the most strangely hot things I'd ever witnessed. My eyes darted back to Lauren for her reaction, but she wasn't giving anything away. Would she like it if a guy did that to her?

Nate leaned back on his hands again. His eyes roamed around the circle, stopping on Mia. "Truth or dare."

"Truth."

It was a good call. I wasn't sure I'd want to do a dare Nate came up with either.

"Okay, Mia. I've always wanted to know…" He took a long pause, which could have meant he was drawing out the tension, but I suspected it was more likely he was struggling to think up a question. "Who would you call to help dispose of a body?"

Mia's face broke out with a relieved smile. She must have been expecting something more revealing. "This is for someone I've killed?"

"Yes. A bloody murder."

"Hmm." She rested her chin on her fist.

"I always help you clean up after parties," Allie offered, making Mia laugh.

"True, but I don't want to get caught, so we'll have to dump the body in the dead of night. Somewhere remote. You don't think you'd get spooked?"

Allie bit her lip, which I took to mean yes.

"Do I have to choose someone real?" Mia asked Nate. "Someone I know in real life?"

He nodded. "Someone who you think would say yes."

"I'd call Josh," Mia said. "No question."

"Yeah," Allie agreed. "You have the best brother. He'd bury a hundred bodies to protect you."

"I'm hoping it's only one, and that I haven't turned into a serial killer?" Mia looked at Nate, who shrugged.

"Plus, Ryder would probably tag along," Allie said. "You could put your feet up and let the guys clean up your crime."

Mia smiled. Guess she liked that idea. "Okay, my turn to pick. I choose tonight's guest of honor. Chloe, truth or dare?"

Chloe sat up to attention. "Truth. I'm an open book. No more secrets ever again."

"How do you feel about what Nate did to your ear?" Kai asked.

Nate laughed. "She loved it. I could tell."

Chloe rolled her eyes, smiling as she looked back at Mia for her question.

"Well, if you don't have any more secrets to uncover, I'll go with another hypothetical. If you had to kiss a teacher, who would it be, and why?"

"Please say Ms. Thompson, and that I can watch," Nate said, which got him a few laughs.

"Ms. Thompson?" Chloe twisted to face him. "Is that who you'd choose?"

"She's the obvious choice, right, guys?" He glanced at Kai, then at me.

"Yeah," Kai answered, and I nodded my agreement, briefly making eye contact with Lauren before she glanced away. Ms. Thompson had the whole naughty librarian thing going on.

"I'd prefer to pick a male teacher," Chloe said, earning a *boo* from Nate. "Probably Mr. Ramirez."

"Or Mr. Jenkins," Allie said. "He's the sexiest."

"No way, Allie." Mia shook her head. "Ramirez beats him by a landslide. He has those vibrant emerald eyes."

Vibrant emerald eyes? I shared an amused glance with Emma, confirming she paid about as much attention to our teachers' eye colors as I did.

"I agree with Mia," Chloe said. "Ramirez it is."

"Fair enough." Allie smiled. "Chloe, who's next?"

Chloe scanned her eyes around us, settling them on me. "Well, I guess I should pick my partner in crime. Jason, truth or dare?"

She looked at me with a devious smile. I drew in a breath before slowly exhaling while I considered my options. I didn't think Chloe would embarrass me by asking about Lauren, but there was always the chance she'd do it out of a misguided belief that she was helping, and I didn't want to risk that.

Of course, the other risk was that she'd dare me to kiss Lauren, but that was something I could handle. Something I'd welcome.

Just the thought I might finally have an excuse to kiss her

sent my pulse sky high. And tonight, my desire to do it was out in full force. She was wearing some kind of lipstick that made her lips glisten, and it was a conscious effort to stop my eyes from drifting down to them whenever I looked at her face.

"Dare."

I kept my gaze on Chloe, trying to ignore the rest of the circle. My heart was hammering. She would dare me to kiss Lauren. I knew it, and I couldn't wait. I forced an impassive expression. I didn't want to give anything away from my reaction.

"Okay." The corner of her mouth quirked up higher. "I dare you to go into the bathroom. Keep the light off so it's pitch-black, and stay there for seven minutes."

My face stayed neutral while I waited for more, but Chloe just grinned at me, not saying anything else.

Did she think I was afraid of the dark? I wasn't. And while standing in a dark room for seven minutes wasn't my idea of fun, it wasn't exactly a challenge.

I stood up, trying to hide my disappointment, and it was only then that Chloe added the rest of the dare.

"And take Lauren with you."

My eyes darted straight to Lauren, but she wasn't looking at me, she was gawking at Chloe. It took Emma nudging her before she snapped out of whatever daze she was in and glanced up at me.

I gave her a small smile, then offered her my hand, which she reached out to meet with hesitancy.

I had to be missing something because it wasn't like this was a big deal. Seven minutes in the dark with my best friend was nothing. We would just talk, and the time would be over before we knew it. If Chloe was trying to play matchmaker, she was failing, because without it being an explicit part of the dare, the likelihood of kissing Lauren tonight was almost nonexistent.

Holding her hand, I pulled Lauren to her feet. Then, ignoring the misplaced chuckles and catcalls from our friends, I gently tugged her with me into the bathroom, closing the door behind us and plunging us into darkness.

13

Lauren

I COULDN'T SEE A THING. Without a window, the tiny slivers of light bleeding through from around the edges of the door were all we had. They offered nothing in the way of illumination.

Our friends had reacted as if something was going to happen in here, but they were deluded. Just being alone in the dark wouldn't make Jason suddenly want me.

He'd dropped my hand as soon as we entered the bathroom. From memory, there was a shower built into the wall, plus a toilet at the back and a sink to its side. But what there wasn't, was floor space. This room hadn't been designed for multiple occupancy.

Jason lowered his voice down to almost a whisper. "I think I got off lightly, as far as dares go."

There was no need to talk at a normal volume since we were less than a foot apart. But standing in front of him like this, with Jason talking so softly, it felt different, exciting, and it was making my heart beat so hard I worried he might hear.

"Yeah. It's not much of a challenge," I said.

74

"It's just Chloe trying to set us up. She thinks we'd be good together." Jason's voice was steady, and though I desperately tried to read into his tone, there was nothing to indicate whether he might agree with her.

"Emma's the same. She's so eternally happy with Kai that now she's on a mission to make me—" I stopped myself.

"Make you what?"

We were already standing so close, but it felt like Jason was leaning in more, as if eager to hear my answer.

I sucked in a breath, but couldn't bring myself to finish the sentence, so I started again.

"Emma thinks we'd be good together too. When we get back out there, pick me as your dare, otherwise she will as soon as it's her turn. And I'm pretty sure whatever she comes up with will involve you. Like I said, she's on a mission, and I don't think she'll stop until we..."

The words had been spewing out, but I trailed off. What was I doing? This was pure self-sabotage. I'd probably just ruined Emma's plan and destroyed my chances along with it.

Unless her plan was already happening? Emma promised she wouldn't dare me to kiss Jason. But arranging for us to be in close quarters in the dark? That might have some merit.

If I couldn't actually see Jason's rejection, it might be easier to handle? The darkness had somehow already made me bolder, and I'd already said far more than I'd intended.

Because now Jason knew Emma wanted us together, and surely he knew us both well enough to know that she wouldn't do anything without me on board?

"Maybe we should give them what they want?" he said.

His words sent an excited shock wave through my body.

He couldn't have meant them the way it sounded, but my brain refused to think up any alternative intentions.

"Make it look like we've been doing more than talking in here," he continued.

My heart plummeted as quickly as it had risen. He was only talking about faking. Of course. That was all anyone seemed to do in this town. But he wanted to mess with our friends, and I wanted to know what he was thinking. Going along with it might be fun.

"How do we do that?"

"Easy. We just need to look a bit disheveled. Mess up our clothes and hair, then try to look embarrassed when we stumble out." Even though I couldn't see it, I could hear his smile.

"Okay, let's do it."

It only took a fraction of a second after agreeing for me to realize how this might backfire. If we walked out of here looking as if something had gone on, Emma might think something actually had.

What if she says something?

I couldn't let that happen. I'd either have to find a quick way to convey to Emma that she should keep silent, or disappoint Jason now by changing my mind.

Jason took the decision away from me by stripping off his t-shirt. He moved so fast I barely registered what was happening, but the sounds and the motions were unmistakable.

"What are you doing?" I was all too aware of his bare chest just inches away.

"Making things look believable."

"By taking your shirt off? You want people to think I'm some kind of animal?"

"You are an animal," he answered in a teasing voice.

I huffed, making enough noise for Jason to laugh in response.

"Oh, come on. You expect me to believe that if you were in here with a guy you liked that you wouldn't be mauling him?"

I had no response to that. Jason was oblivious to the strength of my self-restraint muscle, which I exercised daily.

"You should probably turn your t-shirt inside out too," he suggested, and I could hear him putting his back on.

"I can't do that. What if someone opens the door while I have it off?"

Jason didn't answer me, but a second later I heard the click of the lock on the bathroom door. The noise wasn't lost on our friends outside as laughter and *oohs* from the other side of the door seeped through.

"You don't have to take your top off if you don't want to. But now no one can come in, and it's not like I'll be able to see anything."

He was right, but the thought of standing in front of Jason in just my bra still made me nervous, like I was vulnerable, even though I completely trusted him.

Taking hold of the bottom hem, I peeled my t-shirt up, past my pounding heart and over my head.

The air in the bathroom felt cool against my skin, but it was as if Jason was radiating warmth. Even though I could no longer hear him breathing, and he was standing still as a statue, I could sense where he was and could feel the heat from his body.

Remembering what I was doing, I returned my attention to my t-shirt, turning it inside out and putting it back on.

"So, hair next?" I asked. I wanted to reach out and ruffle my hands through his blond mop, something I'd seen his mom do plenty of times, but I didn't dare, and I'd most likely end up poking him in the eye if I tried.

Jason didn't answer, but I could hear the rustling as he mussed up his own hair. Not that it probably made much difference.

"You're not doing yours?" he asked.

I shoved my fingers into my mane, roughing it up at the roots, then shaking my head.

"Your hair probably still looks perfect, but I think that's about as convincing as we can be," he said.

I wanted to argue. We'd be far more convincing if we let them find us in a compromising position when our time was up. But that would require getting into a compromising position in the first place, and now Jason had locked the door, we'd removed the possibility of being interrupted, anyway.

So instead, all I could come up with was, "You think my hair looks perfect?"

Jason let out a light chuckle. "I'm guessing not anymore." He must have reached his hand out then, because with a better spatial awareness than I possessed, he made contact with my hair.

My body tensed as he ran his fingers through it, then scrunched a handful, no doubt adding to the messiness, before letting go.

It was hard to stop my mind from fantasizing. How at any second Jason could take me by surprise and plant his lips on mine. I willed him to do it, but it didn't happen.

"You should probably smudge off some of your lipstick," he suggested.

I couldn't stop my giddy smile, pleased that Jason had noticed my lip gloss, and that even in the dark he'd remembered.

"Good plan." I pressed my finger against my lips, attempting to wipe some off, but doing it blind, it was hard to tell if anything had rubbed away.

"I can't tell if it's coming off," I told him.

"Never mind. I just thought that would make everyone think—" He paused. "It's a shame. It would've looked good if we could've gotten some onto me."

"I agree."

If we wanted people to believe we'd been making out in here, transferring my lip gloss onto Jason would've been very convincing.

"You don't have the tube, or whatever it is, with you?"

"Nope, I think the only way to get it onto you is direct from my lips." I chuckled because the idea was so preposterous, but Jason stunned me with his response.

"Go for it."

My heart just about burst out of my chest, and my breath caught in my throat as I tried to process what I'd just heard.

Go for it.

I don't think any three words had ever filled me with so much excitement before. Excitement and fear.

My brain double and triple checked I was understanding correctly, but there was no mistaking the meaning. The only way to get the lip gloss from my lips to his was with direct contact.

Jason just told me to kiss him.

14

Jason

GO FOR IT.

My words lingered, heavy in the air, while I waited for Lauren to do something. Or say something.

Anything.

My imagination had gotten the better of me. I'd wanted so badly to believe Lauren might have feelings for me that ran deeper than friendship. The words had flown out of my mouth before I'd considered the consequences.

If she wanted more, I'd handed her the perfect opportunity. Making it clear what I wanted and letting her close the distance if she felt the same. But Lauren wasn't responding at all, and that was almost worse than if she laughed in my face.

I'd shocked her with my suggestion, and now I needed some damage control, because I'd told her she should kiss me, and she obviously didn't want to.

I waited for a few more beats, letting my glimmer of hope completely fade away, until I couldn't bear the uncomfortable silence for any longer.

"I'm sure we're believable enough without the lipstick." My

voice made an excellent attempt at hiding the crushing disappointment, and I was grateful for the darkness. If Lauren could see me, I wouldn't have been able to hide how I was feeling. "How long do you think we've been in here?"

Now that I knew I had no chance with her, standing this close to Lauren was hellish. I still wanted to pull her into my arms and mess up her lipstick for real. The small room was feeling claustrophobic, and I was ready to pick up the shattered pieces of my heart and go home.

"Lauren? You still here?"

Wasn't she going to talk to me at all?

"Um, I don't know." Lauren found her voice at last, but she sounded different. The playful good mood had vanished. "I guess they'll let us know when the time's up."

Unless they were planning to leave us here. See how long it took for us to come out on our own.

I sighed. Standing in silence was too awkward. I'd messed things up and needed to clear the air. To tell her I was only joking, even though that was a lie. But I didn't know how.

"I'm kind of wishing that we'd stuck with the Beast Babe plan for tonight," I said, desperate to fill the emptiness.

"Is being trapped in here with me that bad?" There was teasing in her voice, and I felt a small rush of relief that she wanted to lighten the mood too.

"No, it's fine. Not really that different from the original plan."

"Even though my bedroom's a lot bigger than this bathroom?"

It might be bigger, but it wasn't like we used the extra space. And when we watched movies, our bodies were in constant contact.

In here, we hadn't touched at all, other than when I'd reached out to help muss up her hair. That had been a bad move, but at least I resisted trying for more.

Knowing what I knew now, that would have been an absolute disaster.

But even though we were farther apart, the tension was thicker than it had ever been in Lauren's bedroom.

"We'd be together in the dark either way," I answered.

Lauren didn't respond to my comment, and we went back to the awkward silence. We never behaved like this, never ran out of things to say to each other. But right now, I had nothing.

I leaned against the cool wall tiles and let my head fall back. I was trying to put as much space between us as possible, without making it obvious, but there still wasn't enough air.

"Do you think they've forgotten about us?" Lauren asked after what was probably less than a minute, but felt like an eternity.

"Maybe. We've definitely been here for over seven minutes. You think we should go out?"

"Yeah."

I reached for the lock, fumbling around until I found it, then I twisted it unlocked. There was no reaction from the other side of the door.

"Should we hold hands or something?" Lauren asked. "If we want to make it look like... you know."

I paused. We were about to go out there, pretending we'd spent the past seven minutes, or however long it had been, all over each other. I'd been the idiot to suggest it, but it was a spur-of-the-moment thing that had seemed like a good idea at the time.

"I don't think we need to. It's only a bit of fun. I doubt they'll believe it, anyway. They must know nothing like that would ever happen between us."

I held my breath, waiting for her reaction. That was my damage control. If I made it sound like I believed what I was saying, Lauren would think I'd only been joking about wanting her to kiss me earlier.

"Right," she said. "So let's get out of here."

Readying myself for our friends' reactions, I opened the door, swinging it open.

Nobody laughed at us. There were no *oohs* or *aahs*, no suggestive comments. Nothing.

Because there was nobody here.

"Where is everyone?" Lauren stepped forward. She blinked a few times, and I couldn't tell if it was from confusion, or just in response to the lighting, which, while not overly bright, was still a stark contrast to the bathroom.

I scanned my eyes over the room, surveying our surroundings. All evidence of our friends ever being here was gone.

Instead, there were a couple of gym bags on the floor in front of the couch, with a white envelope on top of each. Next to them was a large cardboard box, and sitting on top of the couch was a pile of bedding.

Lauren must've come to the same conclusion I did, because, while I wandered over to the couch to investigate, she darted straight up the stairs. As expected, the envelopes had our names on. I picked up mine, opening it and pulling out the letter.

At the top of the stairs, Lauren tried opening the door, but of course it didn't budge. She banged on it with her fists. "Let us out! This isn't funny, guys!"

I watched helplessly, preparing myself for Lauren's inevitable mini-freak-out. I'd seen it before, and it was hard to calm her like this. I hated how powerless it made me feel.

"Emma!" she yelled. "I know you're there. Let us out right now! You can't keep us locked up against our will. It's a felony!"

She hammered against the door again, but it was no use. No one was answering.

Unsure how to help, I diverted my attention away from Lauren and back to the letter in my hands.

Jason,

Please don't be mad. I know you told me to stop trying to push you and Lauren together, but Emma was persuasive and needed my help with her plan.

I tried going to your house for supplies, but your mom wasn't home. So we bought a few things and borrowed a t-shirt from Nate. Hopefully you'll have everything you need. It's only for one night.

Emma and Kai will be back to pick you up in the morning. Mia and Allie are upstairs. If there's an emergency, just put the stereo on loud to wake them, but it has to be a genuine emergency, not a pretend one!

Sorry, and good luck!

Love Chloe

I sucked in my breath. This development would've thrilled me at any other time. But not tonight. It was the worst timing imaginable. I finally had confirmation that Lauren didn't see me as more than a friend, and now we were trapped together for the night when all I wanted was to go home and spend the rest of the evening alone with my self-pity.

Lauren stomped down the stairs toward me, then she began to pace. "Can you believe this? I knew Emma was up to something, but locking us in? I can't believe she'd do that!" Her eyes frantically skirted over everything our friends left for us then widened as she met my gaze and stopped still. "You realize they expect us to stay here for the entire night?" She didn't try to hide the panic in her voice.

I nodded, opening my arms. "Come here."

Despite everything, Lauren did as I asked, and after exhaling, she stepped into me. I didn't expect my attempts to calm her to work, but I had to try, so I wrapped my arms around her, holding her still.

"Don't freak out," I said into her hair. "We're here overnight, but there's nothing to worry about. They left us everything we need."

"I'm not freaking out," she murmured, even though her breathing was still too fast.

"Good. You're super lucky if you think about it. Of all the people you could be stuck with, you got me."

She let out some kind of sniffle laugh as she melted into me. "Yeah, I guess it could be worse." I held her until she pulled away, giving me a somewhat awkward smile. Then she frowned. "They took our phones. I feel naked without mine."

I gave her a sympathetic smile while I tried—and failed—not to think of Lauren being naked.

"We still have old-fashioned communication. Here, they left you a letter."

I picked up the envelope with Lauren's name on and

handed it to her. I hadn't recognized Chloe's handwriting, but Emma wrote this one.

Lauren pulled out the letter and unfolded it, before moving away from me to read in private. I wished I could see what it said, because locking us up like this wasn't in Emma's character. She was far more likely to be the victim than the perpetrator of a practical joke.

While Lauren was reading, I opened up the cardboard box, finding it chock-full of provisions. There were sodas, bottles of water, muffins and fruit, and tons of pre-packaged snack foods. We wouldn't go hungry. There was even the random inclusion of a slightly dusty bottle of champagne.

Even if we did want to drown our sorrows, opening this bottle would feel wrong. It looked expensive, something someone's parents had been saving for a special occasion.

Once Lauren finished reading her letter, she scrunched it in her hand. She definitely didn't want me to read it, and I was anxious to find out why.

15

Lauren

JASON WATCHED while I screwed up Emma's letter into a tight ball.

Steadying my face, I gave him a half-smile. My annoyance with Emma wasn't Jason's fault, and I didn't want him to get the wrong idea about how I felt being stuck down here. Because he was right. If I was going to be trapped with anyone, there was no one else I'd rather be with.

"What did Emma have to say?" he asked.

I hesitated, debating how much of the truth to share. "She said sorry, but it's part of her crazy plan to get us to hook up." I laughed like it was the funniest thing in the world. "I swear, that girl is completely deluded sometimes."

Jason nodded, and my heart sank. After a brief moment of false hope in the bathroom, which I'd wasted by turning into a statue, he'd made it clear that nothing would happen between us, and now I was trying too hard to reinforce that I felt the same, but I didn't actually want him to agree.

"Can I read it?" he asked.

My eyes had scanned through the letter. The bubbles of irritation made it hard to concentrate, and now I couldn't remember exactly what Emma wrote, whether she'd put anything incriminating.

"Oh, I've destroyed it now. Can I read yours?"

"You've destroyed it? We can just unscrunch the paper."

"Well, we should destroy it. There's no need to read Emma's ramblings." I shoved the ball of paper into the back pocket of my jeans. "Is yours from Chloe? Can I?" I held out an empty hand.

With a nod, he passed the letter to me, thankfully not calling me out on the unfair exchange. I took it and read through Chloe's scrawl.

Emma's letter hadn't mentioned what to do in an emergency.

"We have a way out," I said. "Let's put the music on loud."

I glanced up at Jason, raising my eyebrows. Why hadn't he mentioned this vital information?

"If that's what you want." The frown on his face made it look like my suggestion had hurt him.

"You don't want to get out of here?"

He paused. "I'm just thinking about what happens next. If we foil the girls' plan, don't you think they'll try something else?"

I sighed. Even though I hadn't confessed, Jason had made his thoughts on us ever getting together clear. Surely Emma would have to ease off now? She wouldn't want me to get hurt, and that was all forcing me to tell the truth would achieve.

"I say we ride it out," he continued. "It's what? Less than twelve hours? And we'll sleep through most of that. Then in the morning when they see we're still just friends, they'll back off. But it's your call. Just promise to let Chloe know whose idea it was to escape."

"Now the truth comes out." I smiled. "You're scared of Chloe."

He shook his head in denial, ending with a slight wince that made me laugh. Chloe could be determined. Not someone it was easy to argue with.

"Okay, we'll stay." I gave him another smile, which Jason returned with his own weak one, like he was already regretting the decision.

But he couldn't have been as conflicted as I was. I wanted to go home and wallow in misery, to stay away from Jason. It hurt to look at him, knowing he'd never be mine.

Yet we were still friends. Even if we couldn't have anything more, actively choosing not to spend time with him was a struggle, and I didn't want to make things weird by acting different from usual.

Jason kneeled next to the bag left for him and opened it up, peering inside. He rummaged around for a few seconds before pulling his arm out and waving a toothbrush. "Chloe bought me the essentials."

Joining Jason on the floor next to the bags, I opened mine and checked inside.

"Is it all your own stuff?" Jason asked.

"Yeah, looks like it. They're so sneaky. Chloe dragged me out of my room to help her choose which top to wear, but she was being tediously slow. That must've been a distraction so Emma could pack."

"You don't mind Emma going through your things? I'm kind of relieved Chloe didn't get the chance to pack for me."

I shrugged. It's not like she'd been snooping, but it was still an invasion of privacy. "We're best friends. I don't have any secrets from her."

I rifled through the bag. Emma had erred on the side of caution, and along with clothes for tomorrow, she'd shoved in two extra pairs of shoes. It wasn't the most considered collection, but she must have packed in a hurry.

"Aren't we best friends too? Would you let me pack for you?" Jason asked.

No way. "That's different."

"Because you have secrets from me?" He raised an eyebrow and had a bit of a smirk, as if he thought he'd tricked me.

I rolled my eyes, not wanting to rise to the provocation and be forced to explain the different dynamic between same-sex or opposite-sex friendships, especially when he was only teasing. "It's just different."

Spotting the old pink hairbrush that Emma packed for me, I grabbed hold of it and stood up, trying not to acknowledge Jason's grin.

"I'm going to fix my hair," I said, before dashing to the bathroom, locking the door behind me and flicking the switch on the wall. An action I regretted as soon as the harsh white light hit my skin and I saw my reflection.

The goal earlier had been to make us look disheveled, but I'd somehow imagined that as flushed with exhilaration rather than looking like I'd just woken up after a night out I couldn't remember.

There were still traces of lip gloss, but most of it was gone, especially from my bottom lip where I'd tried to rub it off earlier. Rubbing some more, and aided by the mirror, I removed the rest of the gloss.

Trying not to think about the situation with Jason, I plunged the hairbrush into my hair, dragging it through until it stopped without warning. I let go of the brush and it stayed where it was. With an annoyed sigh, I returned my hand to the handle and yanked harder, but that did nothing to untangle the mess.

Not wanting to cause myself any more pain, I lifted the brush back out, finding a different section of hair to tame. *Ouch.* It got stuck again.

My hair shouldn't be so tangled after all I'd done was mess it up a little. This was like I'd been through a hurricane. It didn't make sense.

I extracted the brush from my hair, then held it up in front of me for inspection.

It was the one I suspected, and it had caused knots in my hair before, but never like this. But then again, I'd never started with such an existing mess. I thought I threw the brush away after just a few unsatisfactory uses, but I must have shoved it in a drawer somewhere instead. It was pretty impressive that Emma had found it.

Abandoning the hairbrush, I ran my fingers through my hair, fixing it as best I could. I attempted to untangle the knots but reluctantly accepted they'd have to stay until I got home. I'd have to try not to let them irritate me, although, without a hair tie, that might be impossible.

Lastly, I switched my t-shirt back the right way around, then looked in the mirror. I didn't look great, but it was a marked improvement. I was back to normal.

Then, appreciating being alone for the first time tonight, I closed the lid on the toilet, sat down, and took a deep breath.

Things weren't going to plan, at least not my plan. And even though my heart was aching, I wasn't surprised. Jason had all but confirmed he wasn't the slightest bit interested in me, so I needed to try to look on the bright side, even if it felt impossible. At least I'd avoided the humiliation of confessing and the rejection that would have followed. This wouldn't change our friendship.

I retrieved Emma's letter from my pocket, uncrinkling it as best I could. Maybe if it wasn't too bad, I could let Jason read it. He'd looked disappointed that I didn't let him see, and now that he was joking about me keeping secrets, I wanted to prove him wrong.

I read the letter through again, considering all Emma's words and how Jason might interpret them.

Lauren,

I know you must be seething right now. I'm sorry, but please try to hold in your anger and don't take it out on Jason.

We aren't letting you out until morning, so you'll have plenty of time alone with him to talk (or whatever). Make it last!

I know you can do this. It'll be worth it.

Good luck, and I can't wait to hear all the details tomorrow,

Emma

PS, I told your parents that all the girls were having a sleepover at Mia's.

It mostly read like Emma was pushing me toward him. All except the *I know you can do this* line. That implied I knew what she was talking about, like it was something I was actively wanting to do. Nope. I couldn't let Jason read this.

Realizing I'd been in the bathroom too long, I gave myself a final check in the mirror before heading back out to Jason. Emma's plan had failed, but I was still here with one of my best friends, and I intended to make the most of it.

16

Jason

WHEN LAUREN EMERGED from the bathroom, I was halfway through reading the instructions Mia left for us about how to convert the couch into a bed. Her penmanship was even worse than Chloe's and included some drawings. Drawings of stick figures making the bed, rather than anything useful, but they made me laugh.

Lauren had made herself more presentable while she'd been away, which was a shame, but at least it helped keep my imagination in check. I'd taken the opportunity to reverse my shirt, too.

"So, the couch turns into a bed?" Lauren eyed the pile of bedding next to me on the couch. "They didn't leave a separate air mattress or anything?"

"Nope, just this."

It was like a sick joke. After fantasizing about sharing a bed on our road trip, it was actually happening. But not the way I wanted.

Lauren was still staring at the couch like she'd never seen

one before. I frowned. Guess she wasn't fond of the idea of sharing with me.

"I'll take the floor," I said, causing her to snap back to earth.

"What? No. Don't be stupid. The floor looks uncomfortable, and it'll be cold. I don't mind sharing. It's no big deal."

"Are you sure?"

She gave a convincing nod.

I swallowed. Lauren was still my friend. We could share. She was right; it was no big deal.

"What are you reading?" she asked. I answered the question by handing her the sheet of paper.

She laughed as she looked it over, just like I expected her to. "This looks overly complicated, and I can't even read what it says." She handed the instructions back to me. "Good luck."

"You want me to convert it now?"

She nodded. "Yeah."

So I did. Abandoning Mia's instructions, I opened out the couch with ease, then lay down on it.

"That's it? Even I could have done that." Lauren stood over me.

"Are you minimizing my skill?"

She laughed again. Man, I loved that sound.

"It's all good practice," I said. "We have a new neighbor across the street, and I promised to construct some furniture for her."

"An old lady?"

"No." I sat up. "She's probably only a couple of years older than us. But she has a cast on her arm, and she's on her own, so I thought I'd be neighborly and help out."

Lauren nodded and gave a half-smile. "Well, she's lucky to have such a helpful—such a skillful neighbor."

"Thanks." I chuckled. "So, should we make up the bed?"

"Okay, but no snacks on the bed once it's done. I know what you're like and I don't want to sleep in a pile of crumbs."

I pretended to look offended, and Lauren stuck out her tongue in childish retaliation. She'd based the comment on past experiences though, so I couldn't really argue.

We worked together to make up the bed, not even needing words. Once we were done, she sat down, propping a pillow against the armrest before leaning back and stretching out her slender legs. I mirrored her pose, leaning against the other armrest and shifting my legs next to hers, but being careful not to touch.

I hated that I still wanted to. I had to get over this.

"So, what do you want to do now?" I asked.

She shrugged. "How did people entertain themselves before technology?"

"They talked, told stories, played games."

Lauren's expression stayed blank. Guess those options didn't impress her.

"We do have some technology," I said. "The dance floor."

I glanced over to the grid of LED squares in the corner of the basement. It was an impressive setup. I'd witnessed Mia showing off her moves before, and it was clear dancing was her passion.

"Can we even work that without Mia's phone?" Lauren asked. "Not that I want to. At least, not sober."

"Did you see they left us a bottle of champagne?"

"They did? Well, in that case I'll need at least half the bottle."

I laughed, then raised my eyebrows. "So, you're saying you want to get drunk and show me your boogieing skills?"

Lauren was almost as bad a dancer as I was.

She hesitated, as if reflecting on the idea, before grimacing. "So, talking it is."

I nodded slowly, while searching for something to talk about.

"Are you looking forward to Leia coming home?" I asked. Leia was Lauren's older sister, and she'd be home from college for winter break.

"Yeah. She'll be back in just over a week. We should probably try to squeeze in some more movie nights before then. Once Leia's home, she'll only get in our way."

"Sounds good to me," I said.

"I can't believe it's nearly Christmas already. I haven't even started shopping."

"You still have time."

We weren't far into December. I tended not to think too much about the festivities until about a week before, mainly because Christmas was fairly low key in my house. And although I loved Mom, I couldn't help but feel envious of Lauren's big, happy family.

"I guess, but my mom had all her gifts already wrapped by the end of August. What are your plans this year? Are you visiting your eccentric uncle again?"

I sucked in a breath, bracing myself for a dose of pity. "He's out of town, and it looks like my mom will be working."

Lauren frowned, sympathy in her eyes. "Can't she swap shifts with someone?"

"In theory, but a lot of the other nurses have young children, so it's more important they get to be at home." It wasn't worth mentioning that Mom wasn't originally scheduled to work and had already volunteered to swap in order to help a coworker. That would only make Lauren pity me more.

"That sucks. So what are you going to do? You aren't planning to stay at home alone, are you?"

"It's no big deal. It's only one day."

"It's Christmas, Jason! Come to my house."

"Really?" I couldn't stop my lips from twitching up. I'd hoped for this reaction.

"Yes, really! I can't let you stay at home all alone in the cold. Say you'll come?"

The tugging on my lips turned into a full smile. "Why would I be cold?"

"You just would. But not at my house where we'll have a roaring fire. So, can I tell my parents to expect a guest?"

"Maybe you should check with them first?"

I didn't think they'd mind, but this was a family event, and I didn't want to impose.

"Check with them? Seriously? You're practically one of the family. My dad already has names for at least six of our children."

I laughed, even though her joke left a bitter taste. I needed to accept reality, and having to fend off the teasing about our future together wouldn't make that job any easier. "Well, in that case, I'd love to spend Christmas with your family."

She grinned, looking pleased with herself, excited. "Perfect. And your mom should join us too when she finishes work."

"Thanks."

Lauren continued talking, her eyes lighting up as she told me more about her family's plans for the holidays. She was inviting me along to everything, and it was sweet, but overkill. I didn't need to help pick out their tree.

While we talked, she played with her hair, fiddling behind her neck with her fingers.

"What are you doing to your hair?" I asked after she scrunched her face for about the third time.

"Just trying to detangle. The brush Emma packed made things worse."

She winced as she pulled on some strands of hair.

"I can help. Did Emma pack any scissors?"

Giving my leg a gentle kick, she pasted a fake scowl onto her face. "If she did, I'd use them to defend myself. Keep you away from me." She made a stabbing motion with her arm.

I held my hands up in surrender. "Don't worry, I wouldn't dare touch your hair."

"That's not true. You touch it all the time."

"That was before you threatened to stab me," I teased. "But I won't do it again."

She pushed her lips to the side, and I could tell she wanted to backtrack. My heart surged at the confirmation that provided. She liked it when I played with her hair.

"No, it's fine. Just don't use scissors."

"Deal."

I watched as Lauren returned her fingers behind her neck and continued her untangling attempts. I couldn't really see what she was doing, but the annoyance on her face told me it wasn't working.

"You want me to help with that?" I asked. She met my eyes, considering the offer. "No scissors," I added.

She smiled. "Guess it's worth a try. It is kind of bugging me."

"Where's your brush?"

"That's what caused the problem."

Okay, so I'd just be using my fingers.

"Where do you want me?" she asked.

I tried to ignore the way my mind interpreted her question and made my pulse speed up. But the easiest way for me to access her hair was for her to sit between my legs. So I moved one leg to the side and patted the space in front of me. Lauren scooted over, exactly where I wanted her, with no complaint. Then I bent up my knees on either side of her to make things more comfortable.

"Hold your hair up," I said. Lauren scooped her mass of hair into her hands, then held it on top of her head. I gently pulled out the knotted sections so I could work on them without the rest getting in the way.

"Your hairbrush did this?" I had zero experience in girls' hair, but this was more of a mess than I expected. "How is that even possible? It looks like you might have some baby birds nesting in here."

She laughed. "Messing it up in the bathroom probably didn't help. I swear it was fine when I left the house."

I picked at the main clump of hair for a few minutes, trying not to let my hands come into contact with her skin, because whenever they did, there were definite tingles.

In all the time I spent with Lauren, I never missed an opportunity to study her. I knew every inch of her body, at least the parts that were on public display, but this was a new angle.

Now her delicate neck was right in front of me, and I was having to fight the urge to lean forward and kiss it. Or maybe

I would stroke along it with my fingers and embrace the tingles?

The desire to kiss her was the strongest. I would work up her neck, then press my lips behind her ear. Maybe even lick it the way Nate did with Chloe. But whatever option I went for in my fantasy, I couldn't stop imagining her swiveling around and letting me discover her mouth completely.

"Did you do it already?" Lauren asked, and I realized I'd stopped working on her hair.

"Nearly. I was just figuring out which bits are joined up."

Forcing my concentration back onto the task at hand, I pushed all inappropriate thoughts away. It was like something had shifted since the bathroom. Even though I now knew where I stood, I couldn't stop my mind from rebelling. It still wanted me to be tempted, and as a result, that bad part of my mind was working in overdrive tonight. Being stuck together was only making things worse.

It took a few more minutes before Lauren's hair fell apart, tangle-free but a bit worse off from the experience.

"All done," I said, and Lauren dropped the rest of her hair, letting it cascade over her shoulders.

"Thanks. My arms were starting to ache."

She crawled back to her side of the bed, returning to the previous position and facing me. Then she sighed, letting her head drop back on the top of the pillow. "What time do you think it is?" She kept her eyes on the ceiling.

"No idea. Maybe around ten? Are you tired?"

"A little. How are you feeling?"

"I'm happy to hit the sack if that's what you want?"

I wasn't overly tired, but my emotions had been all over the place this evening, and a chance to reflect would do me good. Plus, if I was going to be following obscure furniture-construction directions tomorrow, it was best not to be too sleep-deprived.

Lauren lifted her head to look at me. "You don't mind?"

"No."

Lauren crawled down to the end of the bed, then stretched her arm out and hoisted her bag up. "You want yours too?"

"Yeah, thanks."

She grabbed it and gently tossed it in my direction.

"You can take the bathroom first if you want," she said, opening her bag and rooting through it. "I'm hoping Emma packed something for me to sleep in."

"Please tell me it's those unicorn pajamas," I teased.

She shook her head. "Those are long gone. How do you even remember?"

"You got rid of them?" I let my face drop.

Emma found some pajamas in Lauren's bed about a year ago after complaining she was sitting on a lump. They were pale pink with bright red unicorns printed on, and some glitter thread over the horns.

Emma had playfully teased that they were the height of fashion, and I'd joined in with the banter, even though I was secretly dying for Lauren to model them for me.

Lauren's lips twitched as she took in my disappointed expression, but she didn't answer.

So, as I took the toothbrush and toothpaste Chloe bought for me to the bathroom, it left me wondering. If Lauren had gotten rid of her unicorn pajamas, what did she sleep in now?

17

Lauren

THIS WAS GOING to be a problem.

I cringed as I held up the skimpy red sleep shorts Emma had packed for me. Did she choose these on purpose?

Sleeping in the same bed with Jason was one thing, but I'd expected to be covered up, and these shorts didn't cover much at all.

I'd searched through the bag, and they were my only option, short of sleeping in my jeans. But it was hard to worry about showing off my legs when there was a bigger issue.

I peered back into the bag, biting my lip as I looked at the baggy blue t-shirt which Emma had tossed in.

There was no way I could wear that. Jason would recognize it, and I had no explanation that didn't make me sound unhinged.

It wasn't like I had a shrine to him or anything, but admitting I'd covertly rescued one of his worn-out old t-shirts before it landed in the trash just wasn't an option.

That wasn't something normal people did. But I hadn't been able to resist when the opportunity presented itself, and it turned out to be the perfect sleep shirt. Soft cotton that was loose enough to be comfortable, but not so big that I'd get tangled up. And most importantly, it made me feel close to Jason.

The bathroom door opened, pulling my attention away from my clothing dilemma. Jason stepped out, looking the same, and I wondered what he planned to wear in bed.

I got my answer when he returned to the bed and climbed in, pulling the covers over himself.

"You're going to sleep in your jeans? Isn't that uncomfortable?" I asked, my question forcing my own decision to opt for the sleep shorts.

"It's only for one night, and it's not like I have anything else."

"You could take them off," I said with a half shrug, trying to sound casual, even though my heart was thumping against my ribs. "I mean, unless you're..."

"You think I'm going commando?" Jason sat up, raising an eyebrow as he gave me an amused smile.

"I don't want to think about that," I lied, meeting his smile. "I'm trying to be nice here, Jason. You can be uncomfortable if you want, but you don't have to be. I mean, it's not like I'll even know the difference from the other side of the bed."

Jason looked at me for a moment. "You're sure you don't mind?"

"Why would I mind?"

He didn't answer me. Instead, he reached down under the covers to remove his jeans, which he then dropped onto the floor beside the bed.

My heart was still pounding, even though there was no

reason for it. I'd be sleeping on the other side of the bed. Jason could be stark naked and it would have no direct impact on me. At least it shouldn't, but just the thought was having a definite effect.

"This is much better." He sat up again, then looked at me sitting motionless in front of my bag. "Aren't you going to get ready for bed?"

"Yeah, I'm just working out what's best to wear."

"You have options?"

"No, not really." There was no way I could let him see his old t-shirt. "Emma forgot to pack me a top to sleep in, so I guess I'll stay in this one." I plucked out the sleep shorts and the things to brush my teeth with from the bag.

"But you hate sleeping in tight clothes."

That was true, but it surprised me Jason knew it.

"You could wear Nate's t-shirt? Look in my bag." He tilted his head toward the bag on the floor, which was out of his reach.

I climbed off the bed, walked around to the bag, then pulled out Nate's t-shirt. The front of the green shirt was covered in a design with three golden triangles—most likely something from a video game. But where the design was printed on, the fabric was almost rigid, barely flexing as I touched it.

"I'm not sure about it," I said. "It has the plasticky kind of print, and it's massive. I think it would annoy me. Besides, it's for you to wear tomorrow."

I returned it to the bag. I was being fussy, but the t-shirt I was already wearing was the better choice, even though far from ideal.

"Do you want me to check for peas under the mattress?"

Jason teased, making me laugh. Then, after a moment, he added, "You can wear mine."

My mouth hung open as I froze at his words. His kind offer shouldn't have surprised me, but for some reason, I hadn't even considered it. The thought excited me, and that must've been obvious when my jaw lifted and my lips formed a hopeful smile. Jason shook his head at my reaction, probably wondering why I hadn't just asked.

Then, with no warning, he stripped off his t-shirt, wrapping it into a ball and throwing it at me. Somehow, I caught it, even though all of my concentration was being used to stop myself gawking at Jason's chest.

I'd seen him shirtless multiple times before, and it was always a struggle to keep my eyes off his lean muscles. But something about the unusual scenario, us being all alone, and him sitting in bed, made things feel different—more intense.

"Thanks." I averted my gaze, even though I wanted to stare, wanted to commit this image to my memory. Then, after scooping up the rest of the things to take into the bathroom, I hotfooted it back into that refuge, locking the door behind me.

Inside, I took a deep breath.

How was I going to survive the night, knowing Jason would be a few feet away, in nothing but his underwear? I tried to push those thoughts aside while I shed my outer layer of clothing, shivering from the air, which had been getting colder all evening. But it wasn't like I even had a choice in the situation; we were stuck in here together.

All I had to do was keep my emotions under control until the morning, and then I could go home and try to figure out what to do next. Jason had made it as clear as possible that nothing would happen between us. I needed to accept that, even though it made my heart ache. I needed to stop thinking about him and get ready for bed instead.

Grateful that I'd shaved my legs the last time I showered, I pulled on my shorts. Then, opening up Jason's t-shirt, I took a sniff. Possibly not the best way to help me get over him, but how could I resist? As expected, it had his scent. There was some kind of pheromone magic at play, so I inhaled deeply.

Next, I stared in the mirror at the pathetic sight of myself with my nose buried in Jason's yellow t-shirt, before coming to my senses and putting it on.

Jason didn't care about fashion, so tended to keep clothes until they wore out, and this well-loved shirt was no exception. The fabric was soft from countless washing cycles, and paired with its residual warmth against my skin, it felt just right.

I'd planned to keep my bra on, but now I was having second thoughts. Jason gave me the shirt off his back to make me more comfortable, and I didn't want to make his efforts a waste.

So, before I talked myself out of it, I hooked the straps over my arms, unfastened the clasp, and let my bra fall to the floor. Then I hugged Jason's t-shirt tight against my skin.

After I'd finished with the rest of my bathroom business, I picked up my discarded clothes from the floor and held them against my chest for some modesty.

When I left the bathroom, Jason propped himself up from his lying position to glance over, sending a thrill through me as his eyes rested on my legs. But it was only for a second before he looked up at my face. "You okay to get the lights?"

I nodded, then looked around for a switch, finding one over on the wall opposite the bed. The room went dark when I flipped it. Not pitch-black like in the bathroom, but dark enough that my journey back toward the bed was mostly stumbling. Once there, I dropped my bundle of clothes into my bag, then climbed up, slipping under the covers and staying as far away from Jason as possible.

I stared up at the ceiling, too on edge to sleep. Plus, I needed to warm up first. Even from a distance, I could sense the heat radiating from Jason, but there was no way I'd dare to move closer.

"This is weird, isn't it?" Jason let out a light chuckle.

"Yeah."

"Well, goodnight, I guess. And try not to snore."

I snickered. "Same to you."

We fell into silence after that, and as time dragged on, I decided there was a strong probability I'd lie awake all night. It didn't help that instead of warming up, my legs were still frozen, and even though I kept my socks on, my toes were turning into icicles.

I rubbed my feet together.

"What are you doing?" Jason murmured. He'd been so still and quiet that I'd thought he was already asleep.

"Just trying to warm up."

"You're cold?"

How could he even ask that? It was freezing down here; the heat switched off hours ago.

"Yeah, just a little."

"Come here. I'll warm you up."

There was nothing suggestive in the tone of his voice. If anything, he sounded too drowsy to know what he was saying, but it still made my breath catch in my throat. I couldn't let Jason *warm me up*. The thought of snuggling up against his bare chest got me too excited. There was no way I'd be able to hide how my body reacted toward him, so I couldn't risk getting any closer.

"Don't worry about it. I'll be okay. I'm just being fussy again."

He let out a soft, dozy laugh. "Well, I'm over here if you change your mind."

"Thanks." I shifted toward him a little, but still kept my distance.

"Or we could swap sides," Jason suggested.

That was a tempting offer, but even though his side would be warm when I got there, I wasn't about to leave the bed to walk around. I wouldn't ask Jason to do it either, not when he was so close to sleep. And rolling over him was absolutely not an option.

"No, it's fine." I curled up into the fetal position and hugged my legs as I thought through everything that had happened in the past few hours.

My relationship with Jason was still solid. But even though I now knew how he felt, it was like that still wasn't enough to dissuade me from wanting to make a move.

I was probably some kind of masochist, because I needed things to be more final. I needed to tell him the truth and let him break my heart. Because until then, I still had hope.

And the only way to quash that was to bring on the pain and confess my feelings.

And when you looked at it like that, tonight's events— Emma's crazy plan—had all been for nothing. It hadn't changed a thing.

18

Lauren

I DON'T KNOW what one thing pushed me over the edge and forced me to wake up. But when I did, intense sensations flooded through my body, overwhelming me.

My pulse quickened and my nerves went into overdrive as I took in the situation. Was this real? I pushed my nails into the palm of my hand. Yes, I was definitely awake. It had been worth checking, because this easily could've been a dream. A vivid dream, a fantasy, but I'd imagined us like this many times, and reality had never come close.

We'd fallen asleep side-by-side, not touching. I'd made sure of that. But now we were snuggled up together, and it must have been my fault, because I was on Jason's side of the bed. It was still dark outside, so I had no idea what time it was, but in those minutes, or hours, that I'd been asleep, I'd moved over to him. Not that I blamed myself for my actions while I was sleeping, just like I wouldn't blame Jason for his actions now.

His face was nuzzled into my hair, his lips close to my neck, and he was mumbling incoherent sentence fragments.

He had his arm draped over me, his hand resting flat against my midriff.

No. Resting was the wrong word, because he was moving his hand, brushing it over my skin and leaving a trail of fire in its wake. My t-shirt had somehow ridden up, exposing my bare stomach, and he was taking full advantage of the easy access.

Although I couldn't really consider it taking advantage, because I was ninety-nine point nine percent sure that he was asleep. It wasn't only because of the lazy way he was caressing me, and the soft but unintelligible murmurs, but because there was no way that Jason would touch me like this if he actually knew what he was doing.

Even if in some alternate universe he wanted me, he'd never do anything to a sleeping girl. No way he would touch her without consent.

And while I would willingly give mine, he didn't know that.

My breath hitched as he tightened his grip on me and used his arm to pull my body back against him.

Holy crap. Jason had to be dreaming, and whatever was happening in the dream was arousing him more than I could handle.

"... so much," he whispered as he peppered little kisses over my neck. His aim was terrible and half the time he was catching air, but each time his lips touched my skin, it sent shock waves straight through me.

This was so, so wrong. Jason didn't know what he was doing, and by letting him continue, did that make me the one taking advantage?

"... love you..." he mumbled into my ear. I squeezed my

eyes shut tight, imagining he was talking to me. I wished I could see inside his brain. See what was happening in his imagination. Who was he thinking of? Who was he saying he loved?

Despair hit me. I was relishing the attention, but it wasn't intended for me. Was this all that would ever happen between us?

I needed to stop him, even though the heat was throbbing within me, and my body was screaming for more.

Jason's hand reached the edge of my t-shirt, and after fumbling for a few seconds, he continued his exploration, slipping his fingers underneath and making me shiver as his hand stroked my skin.

He was mumbling something else now. Maybe something about waiting? But my focus was elsewhere. My heart thudded even faster, and I panicked as Jason's hand inched upward.

I couldn't let him do this. I wanted it. I wanted him to touch me. But not like this.

"Jason," I said. But he just moaned in response, and his hand kept roaming, sending the sparks over my skin.

Then, when his fingers tickled even higher, I knew I'd let things go too far.

19

Jason

LAUREN WAS KISSING ME. We were spending the night in Mia's basement, and Lauren had confessed that she wanted to be more than just friends. I'd lent her a t-shirt to wear, but she'd told me we didn't need clothes and had promptly peeled it off. My heart pounded as I reached for her, kissing her passionately.

"I've been wanting to do this so much," I told her, moving my lips to her neck where I showered her with more kisses. "I love you, Lauren."

I'd been waiting to say those words for so long, and she reacted with enthusiasm, telling me she felt the same and pulling our bodies closer together.

"Why did we wait for this?" I asked while I stroked my hands all over her. She shrugged, then moaned out my name when I found a sensitive spot, before coming in for another kiss.

"Jason! Wake up!"

Something hard slammed into my ribs, and my eyes flung open. It only took a split-second for reality to take over. I was cozied up against Lauren, way too close. My face was nuzzled into her neck, and my hand was dangerously near to…

I recoiled, pulling my body away from her in a flash, my hand momentarily getting trapped in her t-shirt, which I'd somehow slipped my hand under.

Mortified, I took a moment to process what was happening. I'd been having an amazing dream, but had I been groping Lauren in real life at the same time?

I slapped my hand over my face as I let out a string of curse words.

"I'm so sorry." I gasped for breath. "I don't know what…"

How could I even begin to apologize?

"I'm so sorry, Lauren. I didn't know what I was doing."

It was inexcusable. I'd been pressed hard against her. I cringed.

I tried to think of the right words to express my remorse while my breathing steadied. Was she going to hate me now? She hadn't said anything yet, and not knowing sent my thoughts spiraling.

How did this happen? It was far from the first time I'd dreamed about her, but to touch her while she was sleeping? I was some kind of monster.

"It's okay." Lauren flipped over to look at me, but I couldn't bring myself to turn to face her. Not that I could see much anyway. My eyes were adjusting, but it was still too dark.

"What did I do?" I was desperate to know how bad things were. She wasn't freaking out on me, so that was a good sign. But still, I needed answers. I was talking in my dream. Had that transferred to reality, too? Did she know how I felt about her? That I'd been thinking of her? Did I tell her I loved her?

"Lauren? Say something, please." My voice was strained.

"Don't worry. You were just being a guy." She let out a low, gentle laugh, and I was struck with so much relief that I wasn't even annoyed at the way she'd drawn out my agony. I released my breath.

Just being a guy? What did that mean? Contrary to what some girls seemed to believe, we could control ourselves. I could control my actions. At least while I was awake. Being a guy was no excuse.

"What did I do to you?" I grimaced.

"Nothing. Don't worry about it. You were trying to get under my t-shirt, but that woke me up, so I stopped you."

I swallowed. I'd more than tried. I'd succeeded in getting under her shirt, and with the way my hand had caught, surely she was aware I knew. But for some reason, she was pretending nothing had happened. Trying to save me from the guilt?

"I'm really sorry," I told her again.

I hated the thought that I might have touched her without her wanting it, but another, more shameful part of me also hated that I'd missed it. I'd finally had my hands on the girl I'd wanted forever, and I'd slept through it. That I was even thinking like this was all kinds of wrong. I groaned. What was wrong with me? "I'm so embarrassed."

"I know," she said, and I could hear her smile. Despite my humiliation, I was glad she wanted to tease me with it. She would make me suffer, but only in a playful way. It could have been so much worse.

She reached her hand out and placed it on my arm, the warmth instantly comforting. "Seriously, Jason, don't worry. You were asleep. I know you didn't mean to do anything."

I nodded, then climbed out of the bed, picking up my pillow on the way.

"Where are you going?"

"I'm going to sleep on the floor." I placed the pillow down next to the bed.

"Are you serious? You'll freeze."

"I'll be okay. I'll use a towel to keep me warm."

I stumbled in the dark through to the bathroom. First, I splashed some water on my face, then I grabbed one of the thick, white towels.

How did this happen?

Once I'd calmed down enough to return, I made my way toward my pillow, close, but not too close, to Lauren.

"I'm not going to let you sleep on the floor, Jason," she said. "It'll be cold and uncomfortable. Come back up here."

I hesitated. The bed with Lauren would also be uncomfortable, just for a different reason.

"Come on," Lauren persisted, patting the bed next to her. "Please don't be upset. We can pretend nothing happened."

I frowned. The bed was far more appealing, but I'd already humiliated myself once tonight. What if I had another dream and couldn't keep my hands to myself?

"It's fine." I sat down on the hard floor, getting myself into position. "It's safer for me to be down here."

"Safer? Don't be ridiculous," Lauren said, and I could imagine her rolling her eyes. "Get back into bed. I trust you."

My heart skipped a beat at her words. She trusted me. That was almost enough to make me smile. I'd never intentionally hurt her, or forcefully cross any boundaries, and she knew it. But I'd already overstepped, and I didn't want to risk it happening again.

But knowing she would keep on at me until I relented, I picked up my pillow, and still clutching the fluffy towel in my other hand, I got back into the bed. I rolled the towel into a sausage and positioned it between us. It wasn't much of a barrier, but it was better than nothing.

Lauren laughed at it. I bit my tongue, letting her laugh as I pulled the covers back over me and the towel. Then I waited for sleep to return.

"Are you still awake?" she asked after a few minutes.

"Yeah."

"Tell me about your dream."

I blinked my eyes back open. Was she being serious? She knew what kind of dream it had been. "No way."

"Why not?"

"Why not?" My jaw dropped open. "You want to tell me about *your* naughty dreams?"

Lauren took a moment before answering, and I secretly hoped she'd say yes. "Just who it was about then? A celebrity, or someone real?"

Relief surged through me. She didn't know I'd been dreaming of her, and I wasn't about to admit it.

"Goodnight, Lauren."

She huffed but didn't question me further.

20

Jason

AS MY EYES OPENED, it took a moment to remember that I was in Mia's basement, and I wasn't alone.

In fact, I was very far from alone. Lauren was practically lying on top of me, with both an arm and a leg hooked over, under the covers. Her cheek was smooshed against my chest, and her hair was splayed out over my arm. I loved the feel of her so close, the weight of her body pressing against mine.

Not wanting to wake her, I didn't dare move a muscle. Then, like a bolt, everything came crashing back—all the shame of how I'd tried to act out my dream in real life. But now, with the light shining in through the small window, everything felt different.

I'd made a towel barrier between us. Lauren shouldn't be draped over me like this. Was it possible it had all been a dream? A dream inside a dream? I could only hope.

She hadn't been mad at me, but that wasn't the type of mortification that just went away.

Please let it be a dream.

I drew my head up, trying to look around for the towel,

my only way to find out if things had been real, short of asking Lauren. And I didn't want to wake her, or ever mention what might have happened. Plus, I wanted to stay in this position for as long as possible, to just enjoy the moment, because it was probably all I'd ever get.

I wasn't sure how long we stayed there, Lauren lying on top of me while I watched her sleep. I pushed aside all thoughts of how creepy I was being and took the opportunity to study her.

Despite the way her face was contorted against me, and my suspicion that she might leave behind a puddle of drool when she eventually lifted her head, she still looked beautiful. She fitted against me perfectly.

My study opportunity was cut short when a banging on the door upstairs caused Lauren to stir.

"Good morning!" Emma's voice came through the door.

Still dozy, Lauren lifted her head up—no drool—and met my gaze, giving me her adorable, lopsided smile.

"I'm counting to ten, then coming in!" Emma yelled.

I groaned. I didn't want Emma to come in and ruin the moment.

Lauren blinked, and as she noticed what position we were in, her eyes widened and she jolted off me. "Sorry." She rolled onto her back, then pulled the covers up over her face as if hiding from me, or from Emma, who I could hear unlocking the door.

"Ready or not," Emma yelled from the top of the stairs.

"Make her go away," Lauren mumbled. "It's too early."

I smiled to myself. Last night Lauren couldn't wait to get out of here, but now she wanted to stay in bed?

Emma was on her way down the stairs, and she

approached a step at a time. Optimism shone in her big blue eyes as she looked us over, staring in confusion at the Lauren-shaped lump underneath the covers.

Turning her attention to me, Emma gave me a smile. A smile that contained so many questions. But when Lauren pulled back the covers, Emma's face dropped. Even though I couldn't see Lauren's expression, I could imagine it.

"So." Emma swallowed. "I'll be upstairs with Kai, Mia, and Allie. You guys come up whenever you're ready to head home."

She bit her lip as she looked at Lauren, before giving me another quick glance and retreating up the stairs.

"You okay?" I asked once Emma had gone. "You're mad at her?"

"Aren't you?" She turned to face me.

I shrugged. I was more annoyed at myself. Chloe too, but at least now she'd have no choice but to drop the subject and stop trying to *help* me with my non-existent love life.

"Let's go home," Lauren said. Then, still under the covers, she crawled over to the edge of the bed so she could reach her bag. "Do you want the bathroom, or—"

"Go ahead."

I watched as she stood and grabbed hold of the bag. Then, after giving me a look that I couldn't quite decipher, she turned away from me and took the bag into the bathroom. I couldn't keep my eyes off her legs as she walked away. She didn't often show off so much skin, and seeing her in my t-shirt? It did something to me that I couldn't explain.

I hoped she'd ask to keep it. Even if I never got to see her wear it again, just imagining would be enough.

As soon as Lauren closed the bathroom door, I flung back the covers. And there it was, that fluffy towel crumpled down at the bottom of the bed, taunting me.

I collapsed back down, my fears confirmed. Was there any chance Lauren wouldn't remember? Or that she'd think it was only a bad dream?

While Lauren was away, I jumped up and got dressed. Then I folded the bedding, hiding the towel in the middle so she wouldn't spot it. I was kidding myself that she wouldn't remember, but if there was even a microscopic chance, I didn't want to leave any evidence lying around.

Once everything was in a neat pile, I restored the bed back to its couch formation before relaxing down on it while I waited.

Lauren didn't take long in the bathroom, and when she came out wearing her own clothes, she gave me a friendly smile. "I'm going to head on up. I need to have a few words with Emma."

"Go easy on her."

"Don't worry, I'm sure Kai will protect her from me."

I laughed, glad she didn't seem to be angry. Then I followed with my eyes as Lauren ascended the stairs, carrying her gym bag.

It seemed as if everything between us was normal, that nothing had changed. And I was going to act like that was the case, even though it wasn't, at least for me.

I'd avoided catastrophe and kept my feelings hidden, and thankfully Lauren didn't seem to suspect that my dream was about her.

And even though, after spending the night trapped

together, I was more tempted than ever; I knew what I had to do.

I needed to keep my feet firmly planted in the friend zone. Lauren had made her feelings clear, and I had no choice but to accept them.

21

Lauren

EVERYONE WAS WAITING in the kitchen when I came upstairs. Kai spotted me first.

"Hey," he said, prompting the others to look in my direction.

Our phones were laid out on the counter, so I picked mine up, hoping we'd never be separated again, and then I fixed my attention on Emma.

"Can we talk in private?" I pushed my phone into my pocket.

Was talking alone even necessary? Everyone here had been in on her scheme. They probably all knew how I felt about Jason.

I clenched my jaw as the sense of betrayal filled me.

"Um, sure," Emma said, so I took hold of her arm and guided her into the nearest room.

But as I let go of her, looking around the room we'd ended up in, a new emotion took over. Because it was here, in Mia's dining room, where I'd confessed to Emma about my plan to get her and Kai together, and that I'd been deceiving her.

I had no right to be angry. She was only trying to help me, the same way I'd tried to help her. So instead of yelling, I took a seat at the table and dropped my head into my hands.

Emma was quick to comfort me, drawing up a chair by my side and giving me a half hug by draping her arm over my back.

"I'm so sorry." Her voice was laced with remorse. "I genuinely can't believe he'd turn you down."

"It didn't get that far." I kept my head in my hands, not wanting to face Emma. "But he made it clear that we'd never be more than friends."

"So he didn't actually turn you down?" The hope in Emma's voice made me turn my head and meet her gaze.

"Please don't start, Em. I need to face facts. I have no chance."

Emma opened her mouth as though she wanted to argue, but then she gave me a sympathetic nod. "Let's go back out. We can talk about this later. You must want to go home?"

She was right. I couldn't wait to go home, where I planned to take a long shower and then crawl into bed to hide for the rest of the day. I followed her back into the kitchen, finding Jason joking with the others. He looked so laid back, like everything had been some fun prank, and like nothing that happened overnight had affected him at all.

"Are you ready to go?" Kai asked us.

"Yeah," Emma answered before turning to Mia. "Thanks again. Are you sure you don't want us to help tidy up?"

"No, don't worry."

"That's why I'm here," Allie said, sharing a grin with Mia before waving us off as we left in Kai's car.

NOBODY SAID much on the drive home from Mia's, and I kept my attention focused out the window until Kai stopped the car outside my house.

"Thanks for the ride," I said.

"No problem."

"You mind if I hang out with Lauren for a bit?" Emma asked him, even though she hadn't bothered asking me.

"Of course not." He gave her a smile that said he wasn't at all surprised by this turn of events. Emma leaned over to give him a quick kiss before saying goodbye to Jason. She hopped out of the car, then walked around to retrieve my bag from the trunk.

After saying my own goodbye to the guys, I followed her to the house. Once inside, we didn't even make it to the stairs before Dad appeared.

"How was the sleepover?"

"It was… not what I expected," I answered, remembering the lie that Emma had told my parents. But I wouldn't go along with it. My parents trusted me, and I didn't want to break that trust over something that wasn't even my fault.

"Why?" Dad asked, lowering his forehead in concern. "What happened?"

I glanced at Emma, whose face did nothing to hide her panic.

"Emma locked me and Jason in Mia's basement overnight." I tried to strip all emotion from my voice, but I couldn't stop the smile from coming through, imagining how Dad would react.

His eyes widened as he turned his attention to Emma, who was cringing, her cheeks already scarlet.

"You did what?" He laughed, his trademark guffaw.

As always, that noise was like a magnet for Mom, and she joined us almost instantly.

"What's going on?" She was already grinning as she looked around at all our faces. "What did I miss?"

"Emma, why don't you explain what happened?" Dad said.

"It was only a prank," she answered sheepishly. "We locked them in the basement, but we left food, and there's a bathroom down there..."

"They locked you in a basement?" Mom asked, looking at me with concern.

I nodded, forcing my expression to stay straight. "It was like a nightmare, Mom. They took away our phones!"

Mom pursed her lips, failing to conceal her amusement, while Dad laughed openly at me.

Emma's jaw dropped. But she shouldn't have been worried. She'd spent enough time around my parents to know they wouldn't be mad about something like this.

"I'm sorry." Emma bit her lip.

"You were locked up with other people?" Mom asked.

"Just Jason," I answered, and even though Dad already knew that, my comment seemed to trigger *Dad mode*.

"Hold on a moment. Are you saying you spent the night alone with a boy? Where did you sleep?"

"The couch turned into a bed."

"So you slept in the same bed?"

When I nodded, Dad turned to Emma, giving her a stern look, holding her responsible.

"It was Jason," she argued. "He'd never try to take advantage of her."

Heat rushed through me as I remembered what happened during the night. But my parents either believed in Jason's upstanding character, or despite the teasing, they thought nothing would ever happen between us, because they accepted Emma's statement without resistance.

Not wanting to be questioned further, I put my arm around Emma and guided her to the stairs. My parents didn't stop us from leaving, although as I made my way upstairs, I realized the real interrogation was only just about to begin.

22

Lauren

"THAT WAS EMBARRASSING," Emma said once we were in my room. "They didn't need to know it was only you and Jason. That it was my fault."

"Sorry. I couldn't resist." I sat down on my bed, and Emma came to sit next to me after dumping my bag on the floor.

"So, tell me everything." She had an expectant grin.

"There's no point. All you need to know is that Jason made it clear nothing would ever happen between us. I don't know what I'm supposed to do now. Just get over him, I guess." That felt impossible.

"But you didn't tell him how you feel?"

I shook my head. "I didn't need to. And I'm glad. Now I have my answer and I didn't have to humiliate myself. We can stay friends. Jason never has to find out I want more. Swear you won't tell him."

"Of course not. But what exactly did he say? Can you give me a verbatim quote?"

"Yes, he said *they must know nothing like that would ever happen between us.*"

Emma scrunched her face slightly. "That doesn't make any sense. Nothing like what?"

"We wanted to make it look like we'd been making out in the bathroom."

She grinned. "I need to hear everything that happened. Please, Lauren."

I sighed, knowing I'd have to let Emma cross-examine me, convince her the situation was hopeless, or she'd never let it rest.

"Okay, fine. So, we went into the bathroom, and it was pitch-black in there. I literally couldn't see anything, just a tiny bit of light leaking in around the door."

Emma arranged herself so she was sitting cross-legged on the bed, leaning forward, as if expecting a riveting story.

"Jason said that Chloe was trying to set us up together, and I mentioned you were doing the same."

"You told him I was trying to set you up?" Emma looked incredulous.

"I only said that because I was worried about your plan and thought this way I could blame you if it all went wrong."

She laughed.

"So anyway, Jason suggested we make it look like something had happened in the bathroom, just to get you guys off our backs."

"Jason suggested it," Emma repeated with a smile.

"So, we turned our t-shirts inside out, and then—"

"Hold up. You took your t-shirt off? In front of Jason?"

"Yeah, but like I said, it was too dark to see anything."

"But taking your shirts off, was that Jason's idea too?"

"Yes, but—"

"What happened next?"

"Next we messed up our hair."

"Did you do your own hair, or did he touch it?"

"I did it. Well, he helped a bit. But that doesn't mean anything, Em. He's always touching my hair."

"I know he is."

I ignored whatever she was trying to imply from that comment, not reacting at all.

"Keep going," she said.

"So, then..." I couldn't tell Emma about the lip gloss, could I? She'd jump to the wrong conclusion, just like I had. "So, we thought it must've been over seven minutes and we decided to leave the bathroom."

Emma frowned. "What were you going to say?"

"Nothing." I couldn't maintain eye contact.

"You're holding out on me, Lauren. What else happened in the bathroom?"

"I don't want you to make a big deal out of it."

Emma shook her head. "I won't."

"Well, you remember I had on that lip gloss?"

She nodded eagerly.

"This was so stupid, but we were talking about how it wouldn't look like we'd been kissing without messing that up."

Emma's eyes widened, but she didn't interrupt.

"And for it to be most convincing, we should try to get some on Jason."

She bit down on her lip, as if the excitement was too much for her.

"So I tried to rub some off my lips, but I couldn't tell if it was coming off, and I made some silly comment about the only way to transfer it being direct from my lips."

I cringed, pausing for a breath.

"You didn't! Did you kiss him?" She leaned in even closer toward me, waiting with bated breath. Her smile lessened when I shook my head.

"So, what happened?"

"He said go for it."

"Go for it?" After a moment's thought, Emma squealed, launching herself at me and squeezing her arms way too tight around me.

"You said you wouldn't make a big deal of it." I extracted myself from her grip.

"It is a big deal! He basically told you to kiss him!" Her frown returned. "But you didn't? Why not?"

"Because I froze. I wanted to be sure I understood him, but then before I could act, he kept on talking, and he clearly hadn't meant it the way it sounded."

Looking unconvinced, Emma chewed on her bottom lip.

"We left the bathroom after that, and when he saw everyone was gone, he said it was for the best, because no one would've believed anything could have happened between us." I looked down at my hands.

"So what else happened? Did you freak out when you saw we were gone?"

"Kind of, but Jason calmed me down."

"How'd he do that?"

"He hugged me." I hoped Emma wouldn't read too much into that either. "Anyway, that's everything that happened."

"You went to bed as soon as you left the bathroom?"

"No. But we were just talking, nothing you'd care about."

"Okay, so what about the sleeping situation?"

The heat was rising back up to my cheeks. Emma would want all the details.

"Spill it!" she demanded.

"It was just awkward. Because of what you packed for me to sleep in."

"Sorry, I was trying to be quick. But I thought Jason would like the shorts." She wiggled her eyebrows up and down.

I swallowed, remembering the way he'd looked at me when I walked out of the bathroom in them. "The problem was the t-shirt."

Emma waited for me to elaborate.

I moved from the bed over to the bag on the floor. Squatting down, I searched through it, pulling out the blue t-shirt Emma packed. I stood and held it in front of my body.

"What's wrong with that? It covers everything," she said.

"But don't you recognize it? It used to be Jason's."

Emma looked blank, despite the fact that she would've seen him wear it on countless occasions.

She shrugged. "Why's that a problem? Guys like it when girls wear their clothes, and if he gave it to you, he clearly doesn't mind. He probably enjoyed seeing you in it. Kai always says I look cute when I wear his hoodie." Emma's eyes glazed over.

"He didn't give it to me. I kind of—" I searched for the right word, "—commandeered it."

"Commandeered? Wait, are you trying to say you stole it? Lauren!" Her eyes widened, and she stared at the t-shirt.

"He was throwing it out. And surely it's better with me than in the trash?"

Emma looked at me with a disapproving smile.

"He doesn't know I have it," I said. "I obviously couldn't let him see."

132

"So what did you sleep in?"

I reached back into the bag and pulled out Jason's yellow t-shirt, holding it up against my body the same way I did before.

Emma grinned. "That one I do recognize. So, he gave you the shirt he was wearing? Or did you somehow steal that too?"

"He gave it to me. Well, loaned it. I'm going to give it back."

"Of course you are," she said, as if she didn't believe me at all. "But if you were wearing Jason's t-shirt, what did he sleep in?"

"Shirtless." Then, before she could ask about his bottom half, and because I'd spotted it out of the corner of my eye, I pulled the annoying pink hairbrush from my bag and waved it in the air. "This was an instrument of torture. It completely tangled my hair, making it much worse, instead of better."

She looked at my hair, which was still messy. Without a decent brush, all I'd done was run my fingers through in a feeble attempt to tame it.

"Your hair doesn't look too bad. You're exaggerating."

"No. It was really knotted." I tossed the brush into my wastebasket. Then, before she asked for clarification, I added, "Jason fixed it."

"Jason fixed your hair?"

I nodded.

"He brushed it for you?"

"No, like I said, the hairbrush was making it worse."

Emma looked skeptical, like she couldn't believe a hairbrush could be that bad.

"So, what? He untangled it with his fingers?"

"Yes. But before you get excited, it didn't mean anything. He was just trying to help me, because that's what Jason does."

"Okay, okay, so how about once you were in bed? Did you talk some more, or go straight to sleep?"

"We didn't talk, but it took me ages to get to sleep. It was too cold, and those shorts didn't help."

"Sorry. But if you were cold, maybe you should've cuddled up with Jason. Conserved body heat and all that." She raised an eyebrow.

"Actually, he did offer. But again, he was just being kind, and he was already half asleep, so he probably didn't even mean it. It wasn't as if he actually wanted to snuggle up with me. But anyway, I said no. I mean, he was practically naked, so I couldn't."

"Practically naked?"

I groaned, annoyed I'd inadvertently told Emma that Jason slept in his underwear. But she didn't dig for more information.

"Okay, so you warmed up on your own?" she asked, and I nodded. "And after that, did you get to sleep, or did Jason keep you up all night with his snoring?"

I drew in a breath. There was no way I could confide in Emma what had happened. That wouldn't be fair to Jason. He'd seemed mortified by his actions, and I was pretty sure he wouldn't want anyone else to know. Telling her would be like a betrayal.

"I slept the whole night. You woke me up by banging on the door this morning."

"Oops. So that was everything?"

"Yes." I nodded, then returned to my place, sitting next to Emma on the bed. "You're all caught up."

"I'm so sorry things didn't work out the way we planned," she said. "But it sounds like you made progress."

"Progress? What are you talking about? Are you forgetting about the most important thing? Jason said nothing would ever happen between us."

Emma pushed her lips to the side. "Let's recap, shall we?" I wasn't sure I had a choice in the matter. "Tell me if I get anything wrong."

Emma held up her fists, then began to speak, flipping her digits up as she counted.

"One, Jason suggested you take your t-shirts off in close proximity. Two, he said you should kiss him to transfer your lip gloss. Three, he gave you a hug to calm you down. Four, he gave you his t-shirt to sleep in. Five, he untangled your hair. Six, he wanted to warm you up in bed. Am I missing anything else?"

She was. She was missing the way he touched me in the night when he'd been sleeping. The way he pressed himself against me and ran his hand over my skin while he murmured in my ear and kissed my neck. But none of that meant anything, because he hadn't intended it for me.

Although when I woke up to find my body draped over his, Jason was looking down at me with a smile. He didn't shove me off. Maybe that meant something?

Emma stared at me, and I had to be blushing. But that stuff was private. And just like she didn't share what she and Kai did when they were alone, I wouldn't tell her anything else about what happened with Jason.

"That's everything," I said.

"I'm so sorry, Lauren. After reviewing the evidence, it's

obvious he doesn't like you at all. I'm truly surprised your friendship has lasted this long."

I gave her a small scowl. "Why are you still ignoring the key piece of evidence? The way he said that nothing would ever happen between us. Like it wasn't even a possibility."

"And he said that immediately after you left the bathroom, right? So a few minutes after he told you to kiss him, and you did nothing?"

Emma watched as my brain connected the pieces.

"You don't think he meant it?" I asked.

She shook her head. "You rejected him. He was probably crushed."

"I didn't reject him. I just—"

I still couldn't believe the way I'd turned into a statue.

"It's the same thing. So, what are you going to do?"

I glanced over at her, unsure how to answer. While we were trapped together, I was so sure of Jason's feelings. I'd convinced myself there was no chance.

But now? Emma's fresh perspective was casting doubt on my assessment. Because I had to admit, there was an abundance of signs he might like me as more than a friend, and they were too compelling to ignore.

And that sent my hope soaring to the clouds. I was powerless to stop it.

"I'm going to tell him."

23

Jason

MOM WASN'T HOME when I arrived back. I went to the kitchen, dropping my bag on the table and starting the search for food. There hadn't been much time in between waking up and leaving this morning, so I'd missed out on all the baked goodies our friends had left for us in the cardboard box. Just the thought of them made my stomach growl.

The best thing I could find was some bread, so I made myself a few slices of toast, then sat down to eat, checking the messages on my phone at the same time.

There was one from Mom telling me she'd switched her shifts yet again, which explained her absence now. The rest were from Chloe.

She was apologizing for leaving me trapped with Lauren and was putting all the blame for the plan on Emma. I sent her a quick reply saying that we could talk later.

Next, after a relaxing shower and getting dressed in clean clothes, I grabbed our toolbox from the garage and crossed the street to Marina's house.

"Jason!" She greeted me with a relieved smile, the gratitude shining brightly in her tired eyes. "I'm so glad you're here. Come on in."

I followed her into the house and wondered, not for the first time, whether Marina was up to the challenge of making this place a home.

In the middle of the room was a large playpen, where the twins were entertaining themselves with soft toys. The playpen was surrounded by boxes, scattered all across the floor. The boxes covered a lot of the stained carpet but didn't do much to hide the paint flaking off the walls.

"I know," Marina said after taking a glance at my face. "There's a lot to do."

I forced a smile. "It'll look much better once you've unpacked."

She nodded. "Problem is, there aren't many places to unpack into. That pile"—she pointed to the giant stack of boxes closest to the front door—"is all the new furniture. The rooms need to be painted too, but that isn't urgent. I would have hired someone to do it, but after ordering new carpet, there isn't much left in the budget. And the carpet was a priority. I just couldn't let the boys crawl over that." She looked down at the floor in disgust.

"When's the carpet being installed?" I asked.

"Upstairs is being done on Monday. I don't have a date for down here yet, because the room needs to be clear, so I thought it made sense to wait until I've moved all the boxes. Of course I booked it before I broke my arm." She grimaced as she looked around the room. "Anyway, I'm storing a ton of my brother's stuff, and once I check the boxes, I was hoping you might help me move most of them into the garage." She paused in question, so I nodded. "I can't tell you how much I appreciate your help. This is worse than I expected. There's so much to do…"

"We'll get it done." I tried to sound cheerful, even though my casual offer of help looked like it would turn into a full-time job. "We should start by making a plan."

"Okay."

Marina took me upstairs, where there were two bedrooms and a bathroom. After a quick look around, I suggested that making the upstairs livable should be our top priority, beginning with the painting today.

Marina nodded, happy for me to be the project manager. "You should probably get changed first. I don't want you to ruin your clothes."

Promising I'd be right back, I jogged across the street to my house. I had some old clothes saved for messy jobs like this, but all I could find was my already-paint-splattered old jeans. Not wanting to spend all morning searching for the t-shirt I thought I'd saved, I picked out the oldest one from my closet. That would have to do instead.

When I got back to Marina, she'd also changed her clothes and was carrying one of the boys in her arms. He was quiet, but it looked like I might have just missed some wailing.

"Are you okay to get started without me?" she asked. "Alex is being a tad fussy."

"Sure. Stay with the boys as long as you need. I've got the painting covered."

"You're a lifesaver. Seriously, Jason. I don't know what I'd do without you."

I flashed her a smile before heading upstairs and starting work.

Painting was easy, and using a roller, it didn't take too long to get most of the walls covered in the first room. It wasn't enough of a distraction from reality though, leaving my mind free to relive everything that happened in the basement.

After a while, Marina came up to help, finishing around the edges with almost limitless patience and attention to detail. She offered to order pizza for lunch, and since I'd never met a pizza I didn't like, I agreed.

Once it arrived, I devoured my half of the pepperoni pizza while Marina asked me a few questions about life in Haven Valley. I wanted to hear about living in Los Angeles too, but all her answers were vague, and it was clear she wanted to look forward, not back.

After lunch, I returned to painting, and over the course of the afternoon I got the first coat on the walls of both rooms.

Marina helped when she could, but the twins kept on demanding her attention, so mostly I was on my own. I considered starting on the second coat, but we were almost out of daylight and there was only so much painting I wanted to do in one day. So instead, I cleaned up the roller and the brushes in the bathroom sink, then went downstairs to find Marina sitting in the playpen with the twins.

She reiterated how much she appreciated my help, then we made plans for me to come back over tomorrow afternoon to finish painting the bedrooms. I was more than willing to help, but there was so much to do, and it was going to take time. Time that I'd otherwise mentally assigned to watching movies with Lauren.

But maybe it was for the best. While I loved our private

movie nights, those were the times that we were physically closest.

And now, knowing where I stood with her, snuggling up together was probably the worst thing to do. I didn't need that kind of temptation, to keep torturing myself. Instead, I needed to take a step back. I needed to keep my distance.

24

Jason

I WOKE up early the next morning and dragged myself out of bed to go for a run. I'd had a great routine over the summer, running almost every day. But once school started up, I'd lost my motivation.

It was back again now, in part down to the way Lauren's eyes had flitted over my bare chest. I wasn't normally self-conscious, and the daily body weight exercises I did made sure I wasn't too scrawny.

But when she'd looked at me, I wished I'd put in even more effort to stay fit. So, here I was, back in the park I'd visited so often over the summer, the one where I'd agreed to be Chloe's fake boyfriend. Something that all seemed so stupid now.

I was meeting Chloe by her usual bench again today. She'd sent me more messages last night, asking to see me, and while I was still annoyed at her, I wasn't one to hold a grudge. So I mentioned my intention to come to the park, and she'd insisted we meet.

I still hadn't canceled the plans to watch movies with

Lauren tomorrow. It was a bad idea to go, but I didn't want to disappoint her.

I ran four laps around the park, but my body wasn't used to the cold, and being out of practice, my time was disappointing. For my final lap, I jogged past Chloe on her bench, and she gave me a wave. Then, once finished, I walked back over to join her.

She stood up and pulled me into an unexpected hug.

"I'm so sorry, Jason. I hate that you're mad at me. After everything you did for me, I wanted so much to repay the favor."

"I'm not mad." I pulled away. "But hopefully now you'll give up on the idea of me and Lauren."

"So, nothing happened in the basement?"

I scowled. Her question didn't sound much like giving up on the idea. But she could ask all she wanted. I wasn't about to give her the full recap.

"Don't give up on her," Chloe said. "If you feel the way I think you do?"

I groaned. "Chloe, I already told you—"

"I know what you've told me. But this is me telling you. All I did was help arrange things with Mia and buy you a toothbrush. Emma planned everything. It was all her idea."

Yeah, I was kind of annoyed at Emma, too. Being held captive with Lauren wasn't exactly a hardship for me, but I didn't like people playing games with us.

"You get what I'm saying?" Chloe asked.

"Blame Emma, yeah, I get it. But Lauren's probably already given her a piece of her mind. I doubt she'll be let off easy."

Chloe shook her head. "You don't get it. I swear you can be so clueless sometimes, Jason."

I wanted to be offended by her insult, but she'd softened her voice, and said it with such motherly affection that it was hard to feel anything other than confusion.

"What don't I get?"

She sighed. "Think about it. Do you really believe Emma would go to all that effort if it wasn't what Lauren wanted?"

I scratched at my neck while I mulled over her words. Chloe watched me with a concerned, yet hopeful expression, staring as if she could see the cogs turning within my skull.

Emma was head over heels for Kai. It wasn't a stretch that she'd want that for her best friends too, so her playing match-maker wasn't a surprise. Lauren knew Emma was trying to set us up. She'd told me about it. But knowing wasn't the same thing as wanting it.

I shook my head. "Lauren freaked when she found out we were trapped. Trust me, she didn't want to be there."

"Maybe she was just scared."

"Scared of what? Of me?" My mouth dropped open.

We'd been close friends for years. Lauren wasn't afraid of me. There was no way that was true.

"Not of you. Just of talking to you."

Chloe wasn't making any sense. She thought Lauren was scared of talking to me?

"I've already said too much," Chloe said. "I just want to help you, Jason, and you're both so—so frustrating." She took a step back. "Just think about it, please? See you tomorrow?"

I nodded. Then, after watching Chloe walk away, I jogged back to my car, unable to stop thinking about being in the basement with Lauren, and about my conversation with Chloe.

The thoughts whirred around my mind while I showered and ate lunch, and then all afternoon as I put the second coat of paint on Marina's walls.

The one thing I kept coming back to was Chloe's comment about Emma setting us up.

If Lauren knew Emma's intentions, it was hard to understand why she wouldn't have put a stop to it. Because if there was one thing I was sure of, it was that Emma wouldn't do anything against Lauren's will.

And once I was fixated on the idea that Emma was trying to help her, and that Lauren deliberately hadn't stopped things, I couldn't shift it.

And I didn't want to.

Because that would mean Emma knew what Lauren wanted.

And that what she wanted was me.

25

Lauren

"WE NEED A PLAN FOR TOMORROW," Emma said.

My parents were hosting poker night tonight, and they'd asked me to make myself scarce. So, like every time they hosted, I was spending the evening hanging out in Emma's bedroom.

"Really, Em. You want to talk about this again?"

"Yes. You need a foolproof plan, or you'll never go through with it."

I sighed. I'd failed to convince her when I said I was going to tell Jason. But I meant it. I couldn't continue on this rollercoaster for much longer, slowly driving myself crazy. This time, I was determined. I was definitely going to do it.

And the more I thought about everything that happened in Mia's basement, the more excited I got, because it was easy to believe that maybe Emma's analysis was right. Maybe I did have a chance.

"My plan is to tell him. It's not like I can use a script. But I swear I'm going to do it this time."

"If I had a dollar for every time you've said that I'd be lying on a beach somewhere right now."

"I know, I know. But this time I mean it. And I can prove it." I took a deep breath. "If I chicken out of telling Jason tomorrow, you have my permission to do it."

Emma gawked at me. "Are you serious?"

"Yes. Because it won't come to that. I'm really going to do it this time."

Her expression morphed into a grin. "I'm going to need that in writing."

I laughed, but due to my excited nerves, it came out as more of a giggle.

I was finally going to confess my feelings, and the threat of Emma telling him would be added encouragement. It would ensure I didn't wimp out.

Emma jumped up from her bed and wandered over to her desk. She found a notepad and a pen, then returned to the bed, offering them to me.

"This is for my safety," she said.

I rolled my eyes as I took the items from her, then began to write.

"Wait." She reached out her hand and placed it on mine, stopping me still. "Why don't you write to Jason instead? That way, if you chicken out, I can give him your letter."

There were countless ways for me to confess my feelings, and I'd considered all of them. Writing a letter was a classic, and I'd even drafted a few emails in the past. But it just wasn't my style. I didn't want to put that kind of pressure on him. Emma telling Jason I liked him was one thing, but pouring my feelings out on paper? That was too intense.

"No. In fact, this whole thing is stupid." I let the pen drop from my fingers. "I won't forget this conversation. I promise not to get mad at you. And there won't even be anything for me to get mad at you for, because you won't need to tell him. I won't let it come to that."

"Okay." Emma looked a touch intimidated by my firm tone. "So, you're going to tell Jason tomorrow when he comes over to watch your movies. And if for any reason you don't—"

"Excluding natural disasters, things outside of my control. This is only if I'm too spineless."

She smiled. "Right. But you're not spineless. You're one of the bravest people I know. You just have a weak spot when it comes to Jason."

I smiled at her compliment. Emma suffered worse nerves than I did, but I was far from fearless.

She picked up my pen, twirling it around her fingers. "So, if for any reason you're too scared to tell him tomorrow night, then you want me to do it. Correct?"

I gave a small, sharp nod.

"That's settled then." She grinned. "And no more talking about Jason until you update me after he leaves tomorrow. I can't believe this is finally going to happen."

Finally was the right word. Emma was an incredible friend, and she'd listened to me saying the same things for years without complaining.

But now it was time. I was on a mission, and nothing could stand in my way.

I was finally ready.

26

Lauren

MONDAY WHIZZED ALONG AT LIGHT-SPEED, and it also went painfully slow.

I was more determined in my quest to tell Jason than ever, and like a pressurized container, full of excitement, I was ready to explode.

Because one way or another, everything was going to change tonight. I'd been waiting for this moment forever, and now it was nearly here.

I had a few minutes alone with Jason before we picked Emma up in the morning, but he spent the time telling me about his new neighbor and all the work he'd inadvertently signed up for, and how it might mean fewer movie nights.

That wasn't a good sign.

All day, there were comments and questions about us being locked up. People considered it an impressive prank, and I was happy to go along with their laughter, without revealing too many details.

I should have seen Jason at lunch, but I skipped it. My stomach had been churning all day, and the thought of food made me nauseous. I didn't see him again until the car ride home.

"Everything okay?" He glanced sideways at me after we dropped Emma off. "You're being quiet, and we missed you at lunch."

"I just wasn't feeling well."

"Oh, I heard there was a bug going around. Are you any better now? Want to postpone tonight?"

"I'm fine now." That wasn't exactly true, but knowing I was suffering from nerves, at least there was an end in sight, and I wasn't contagious. "Besides, we can't postpone again, or we'll never get all the movies watched before the festival."

Jason laughed. "That would be a tragedy."

"Yes, it would." I gave him a light punch on the arm. I'd never been able to resist an opportunity to reach out and touch him.

"So, Marina got some new carpet today, and I promised to go over to help build some furniture."

"Tonight?"

He nodded. "It shouldn't take too long. But she's drowning in boxes and really wants some furniture to unpack into."

It was wrong to feel jealous, but I couldn't help it. "So you'll be late coming over?"

Jason picked up on my tone, glancing over at me. "I'll try not to be. I know you want to squeeze two movies in tonight."

"If we can."

Two movies and a confession.

"The Beast Babe," Jason said, flashing me a smile that could melt hearts. "I'm looking forward to it."

"Me too."

THE MOMENT JASON dropped me home after school, I entered panic mode. The homework that was crying out to be completed didn't even get started.

Eventually, I flopped down on my bed, unwilling to do anything other than daydream about how things could go right.

Because I was ready for this. I was prepared.

I'd already showered and brushed my teeth. Then I spent far too much time choosing what to wear, settling on my favorite blue jeans and a lightweight sweater. I even attempted to style my hair, but it was so subtle I doubted Jason would even notice.

And now all there was to do was lie back and wait for him to arrive.

The buzzing of my phone startled me, and I scrambled to pick it up.

EMMA

Good luck! Remember I want all the juicy details as soon as he leaves!

I smiled at her optimism but didn't reply. Instead, I lay back down, returning to my dream world, where Jason returned my affections. My phone buzzed again.

JASON

Sorry, will be late. Furniture taking longer than expected

This was prolonging the agony, but I'd expected it.

LAUREN

No worries. See you later

With added time to kill, and my phone in my hand, I pulled up the photos app and scrolled through.

I paused on a picture from my birthday last year. Jason had wrapped his arms around me for the photo, and it was so easy to imagine that we were more than friends. *If only it were real.*

Then, once I'd stared at my favorite photos of Jason for long enough, I abandoned my phone and returned to fantasizing about tonight.

There were so many variations, so many things I could say or do. I imagined launching myself at him as soon as he stepped into my room. Kissing him and waiting for a reaction. But deep down, I knew I wouldn't be able to do anything that wild.

My phone buzzed for the third time tonight, drawing me out of my thoughts.

JASON

Leaving now

Just reading his message quickened my pulse. After a pit stop in the bathroom, I went downstairs, where I grabbed some sodas for us out of the fridge. I took them back up to my room, checked my reflection in the mirror for the last time, then returned downstairs to wait by the door.

"You look pretty tonight," Mom said. She looked me up and down. Somehow she could sense I'd made an effort, even though I didn't really look any different. She focused on my face. "Although you're a little pale. Are you feeling okay?"

"I'm fine."

"Are you sure? I noticed you didn't eat much of your dinner." Mom put her hand on my forehead. "You don't have a temperature, but maybe you should cancel Jason tonight. Get some rest."

"No," I answered forcefully, before relaxing my voice. "I'm fine, really. Besides, he'll be here any minute." I gave her a smile, but Mom could tell something was going on. She knew me too well.

"If you're sure..."

"Thanks, Mom."

She left me alone, and Jason arrived a few minutes later.

"Hey," I greeted him. "Let's get upstairs quick before my parents try to talk to you."

"Sure." He quirked his lip in amusement, then followed as I sprinted upstairs.

Once in my room, I shut the door behind us.

"Was that about Christmas?" He dropped onto my bed, shuffling back and leaning against the pillows, straight into the movie-watching position.

"Christmas?"

I was so tempted to crawl over to him, surprise him with a kiss. But I wasn't dreaming anymore, and the real Jason would probably have a very different reaction than the one in my imagination.

"Yeah, did you get a chance to ask about me coming over? I thought they'd want to tease us about having mistletoe every-where or something." His eyes twinkled with mischief.

"Oh. Sorry, I forgot all about it."

Jason's smile dropped slightly.

Will he still want to spend Christmas together if he rejects me?

That would be uncomfortable for everyone, and imagining

it briefly made me reconsider my confession. I hated the idea of Jason spending Christmas alone.

But Emma wouldn't let me get away with that excuse. I had to do it.

I climbed onto my bed, sitting next to Jason, then I switched off the light with my phone and started the movie that was already cued up.

Jason threw his arm over my shoulder, the way he always did, gently pulling me into him.

"You promise this is going to be better than the first one?" he said.

"That's what people are saying, but I'll await your expert judgment." I gave him a smile, trying my best to hide my nerves as the movie began.

I lasted about five seconds before I grabbed the remote control and hit pause.

"Can we talk?" I blurted, sitting up straight enough his arm dropped off me, then twisting to face him.

"Right now?" Jason raised his eyebrows. "Don't you want to watch the movie?"

"Yes, but there's something I wanted to talk to you about first."

And then there was silence. Jason stared at me patiently, his face lit only by the glow from the TV. I'd rehearsed the words I wanted to say, but even after swallowing, I couldn't get them to come out.

"Actually," he said. "There was something I wanted to ask you."

A shot of relief hit me. "There was? Go ahead."

"I've been thinking about what you told me in the base-ment, about Emma wanting to get us together."

His words took me by surprise. I'd been so grateful for the reprieve, I hadn't even considered what Jason might want to ask.

"Okay?"

"If you knew what she was trying to do, why didn't you tell her not to?" His eyes roamed over my face as if trying to read into any reaction.

"I didn't know she was planning to lock us up together."

Did he know? Did he know the reason for the plan?

"But you were expecting her to do something, weren't you? That's why you warned me about her picking you in truth or dare?"

My breath caught in my throat, and my heart galloped. He was right, but I hadn't worked out a lie, an explanation to cover for this. So, I gave the only answer I could come up with. The one that scared me the most.

The truth.

27

Lauren

I SUCKED IN A DEEP BREATH, then let the words rush out. "Emma knows how I feel about you."

I met his gaze, and my entire body tensed while I waited for his response. In all the scenarios I'd lived through in my dreams, this wasn't ever how I'd given my confession. And from the lack of reaction from Jason, maybe it wasn't clear.

I forced myself to maintain eye contact. "I really like you, Jason." I couldn't breathe, and my heart was hammering so hard he must have been able to hear it.

"You like me?" His voice was quiet and kind, and he raised his eyebrows slightly. But it wasn't from shock. It was almost as if he looked hopeful.

All I could do was slowly nod my head.

"You mean more than friends?" he asked.

I nodded again, this time able to exhale the air from my lungs.

Jason stared at me for a long moment. He was still so calm, but he understood. He finally knew how I felt, yet he wasn't reacting, and it was torture.

Then his lips curved up into an almost-too-casual smile. "I really like you too."

"You do?" My own nervous smile spread across my face. "For real?"

I had to be dreaming. This couldn't be happening.

"Yeah." His voice was low.

While my brain worked on letting this earth-shattering news sink in, Jason lifted his hand up to my face. He curled his fingers under my chin and stroked over my cheek with his thumb. He'd touched me plenty of times, but never like this, never with this tenderness.

He studied my face. "Are you going to freak out if I kiss you?"

My heart pounded. I wasn't sure I could handle this, and Jason must have thought the same. The emotions flooding through me were too strong. The excitement was too much to contain. But Jason had asked me a question, and I'd been aching to kiss him for so long, I wouldn't miss the opportunity. Not this time.

"Go for it," I whispered.

A grin spread over his face, and he leaned in, softly pressing his lips against mine.

The kiss was brief, and even though I was craving so much more, it was absolutely perfect. Enough to show me he cared, and enough to bring me back to reality.

Jason pulled away with a smile. There was so much I wanted to say and do that the choices paralyzed me. But when his gaze flicked back down to my lips, I knew what to choose first.

Our first kiss had been over in a second. It wasn't enough. So I reached my hand up to the back of his neck, then I closed the distance, leaning forward until our lips touched again.

The kiss was slow, cautious. Jason brushed his lips over mine so gently, teasing as he ignited all my nerve endings.

Even though I intended to stay steady and controlled, I needed more. I'd been waiting for what felt like a lifetime for this. I was desperate to taste him, so unable to fight the urge, I pulled down on his neck, bringing him even closer into me.

Jason didn't try to resist, and instead he encouraged me as our lips parted and I deepened the kiss. He wrapped his arms around me, pulling me in as close as possible while we were still awkwardly sitting on the bed.

The heat spread like wildfire through my body, and a part of me still couldn't believe this was actually happening.

He feels the same!

It was everything I hoped for. All my dreams were coming true.

But then, all too suddenly, he let me go.

"I can feel your heart racing," he said through a smile. "Relax. It's only me."

Only him? I wasn't sure why Jason expected that to calm me, as if he had no clue how much he affected me. I returned his smile and pretended to compose myself, even though it did nothing to subdue the pounding in my chest.

"I'm okay," I said, but I wasn't ready to stop. I'd wanted this for too long, so, keeping things slow, I pulled him back toward me, and then I kissed him again.

28

Jason

LAUREN WAS KISSING ME. We were spending the evening watching movies in her bedroom, and Lauren had confessed that she wanted to be more than just friends.

And this time, I was wide awake.

"I can't believe you like me too," she whispered in between sweet kisses.

"What can I do to convince you?" I stroked my thumb along her lower lip, and she trembled in response. It made me feel so powerful. But it also made me want to protect her, not overwhelm her, so I moved my hand away.

Even though I wanted to kiss her over and over, there was no rush. We had forever, and I wanted to do this right.

"We should calm down," I said. "Do you want to watch the movie?"

She nodded, so we moved back against the pillows. I wrapped my arm around her, pulling her in closer than I'd ever dared before. She snuggled right up against me, then hit play on the remote control before placing it down. I took the opportunity to take hold of her hand, slipping my fingers through hers.

She wanted this too.

Even though it was new and exciting, there was something instantly comfortable about this sensation. Something familiar, and I loved it.

Satisfied, I focused my attention on the TV, trying not to obsess over the feel of Lauren so close.

The Beast Babe turned out to be an improvement over the original. For a start, they'd upgraded the costumes, and even though they were probably still wetsuits, it wasn't as obvious.

The story was pretty much the same, but with the addition of a subplot revolving around our title character aggressively pursuing a romance with the original Beast. Meanwhile, they were working together to scare away the unlucky people who dared to enter their pond.

I made a few of my typical comments, but Lauren didn't offer much response, preferring to stare straight ahead, so I stayed silent for the rest. She still looked content though.

Eventually, the Beast and the Beast Babe smooshed their ugly rubber masks together into a kiss, and the movie drew to a close.

Lauren stopped the movie before shifting to look at me, remaining in my arms.

"What's the verdict?" she asked in a casual tone.

"It was better. They obviously had a bigger budget for this one. The romance wasn't entirely believable, but overall I'd call it an improvement. This is the movie that's expected to win? You think it lived up to the hype?"

Lauren shrugged, and a light blush rose over her cheeks.

"If I'm being honest, I wasn't giving it my full attention. I was kind of distracted."

"Did you follow it at all?"

"Not really." She looked down, as if embarrassed.

I laughed at her admission. "What were you distracted by?" I twisted to face her and moved my hand to rest on the back of her neck.

She smiled at my touch. "I was just thinking. What happens next?"

She looked nervous, and I felt a twinge of guilt for leaving her with questions. I should've predicted this. Lauren had a tendency to overthink, while I was happy to take it easy, let things progress naturally. I was fairly confident we were on the same page, but I guess she needed more assurances.

"Do you want to…" she started. "I mean, when we go to school tomorrow, will we—do you think we should… I just wasn't sure if you'd want to—"

She snapped her mouth closed, and I grinned, not used to seeing her like this.

"We should make things official."

Her eyes lit up. "Yeah?"

"If you want to? Be my girlfriend." I intended it as a request, but it sounded more like a command.

But either way, she gave me a wide smile, gazing at me as she nodded.

I moved my hand around to her face, trailing my fingers over her skin. She looked so beautiful, and I'd been fighting the urge to kiss her again for the entire movie.

And now I'd fulfilled my commitment of watching at least one of her terrible movies, I didn't intend to wait any longer.

Although Lauren was even more impatient, and before I had a chance to act, she leaned forward and gently captured my lips with hers.

I smiled against her as I returned the kiss. This all felt so new, so different.

So right.

29

Lauren

"WHAT ARE YOU SMILING ABOUT, SMILER?" Dad asked, raising an eyebrow as he joined me in the kitchen.

I was re-reading the messages Jason sent me first thing this morning, and apparently I was smiling. It was hard to hide my emotions when I was feeling so blissfully happy, but I pulled in my cheeks a little so I didn't look like a complete grinning fool.

After Jason left last night, I stayed in my room and called Emma. She'd been eager to hear all the details, but beyond telling her how I'd confessed, and that Jason felt the same, there wasn't much else to say.

That we'd abandoned the idea of a second movie, opting instead for more kissing, could be summarized in one sentence. The details of that would stay between me and Jason. Not that anything shocking happened. Although we didn't discuss it, there seemed to be a mutual agreement to take things slow.

I hadn't seen either of my parents until this morning, and

Mom had been rushing out the door, so it hadn't been the right time to break the news of my new relationship.

And now, I was growing more and more anxious about their reaction. They teased me so much about Jason, but I was worried once they found out we were actually together, they might crack down. And all the freedoms I was accustomed to, like being allowed Jason in my room with the door closed for hours at a time, might not stay in place.

Dad was still looking at me, waiting for an answer, but I couldn't tell him what had made me so overjoyed. Even if I were ready to tell my parents, I wanted to do it while they were together, for fairness and to get the best reaction.

"Good night with Jason?" he teased. "He must really like you to sit through those awful movies."

I laughed nervously, but his words gave me pause. Jason always referred to my movies as *terrible*, and there was no way he'd pick them if given a choice. Which meant he was watching them for me. I'd always thought it was just him feeling sorry for me, and being a good friend, but maybe there was more to it than that.

I was hit with a sudden need to know how long Jason had liked me for, because we'd been watching my movies for years.

I wished we'd talked more last night. Not that I had any complaints, but I still had so many questions that needed answers.

"Jason enjoys them. At least he enjoys making fun of them," I said.

"Don't we all? Making fun of them, and their fans." He grinned, so I stuck my tongue out in retaliation. "But it's good to have him back. When's your next session?"

Dad knew about my intention to watch all the festival nominees before they gave out the awards.

"We haven't arranged one. Jason's kind of busy at the moment helping his new neighbor. Plus, we have road trip planning at Emma's tomorrow."

I'd invited him to come back tonight, but Jason had already made plans to help Marina. My jealousy was unjustified, but I still hated having to share him.

I'd even offered my assistance—not that I was the neatest with painting—but Jason teased I would be too much of a distraction. We agreed it would be best to just let him get the job done, and then after that I'd finally have him all to myself.

My phone buzzed.

JASON

Outside

It was only one word, but it still brought my grin back with a vengeance.

"My chariot awaits." I glanced up at Dad, who was watching me. "Later."

I left as quickly as possible, before Dad could comment on my reaction to Jason's message, which he clearly witnessed.

Throwing on my coat and grabbing my backpack, I ran outside, down my driveway, and slid into Jason's car.

"Hey," he greeted me, his eyes sparkling. His car was toasty, but it was the way he looked at me that was spreading warmth through my body.

"Hi." I returned his smile, and we looked at each other for a beat too long before he diverted his gaze to my house.

"Your dad's not coming out? I thought he might want to threaten me or something?"

I laughed. "No." That wasn't something I could imagine happening.

"So your parents took things well?" He started the short drive to Emma's house.

"I didn't tell them yet."

Jason gave me a questioning sideways glance.

"I didn't get a chance. I'm going to, of course. I'm just worried they might come up with rules."

"Rules," he repeated. "You mean like not letting me in your bedroom anymore?"

"Yeah, exactly. Stuff like that. I'm fairly sure my dad doesn't actually want lots of grandchildren. At least not yet. And if he thinks there's a risk…"

I swallowed, uncomfortable with the implication, but Jason just flashed me a smile.

"I don't think we need to worry," he said. "Did they make up rules for Leia?"

"No, but she's never needed them."

Jason nodded in understanding. I loved my sister, but Leia wasn't exactly a boy magnet.

"I'll tell them," I said. "Did you talk to your mom?"

"Not yet, but she'll be happy. Guess our friends will be too. You already tell Emma?"

Jason glanced at me again and I nodded. We'd be at Emma's soon, and then he'd find out just how excited she was about our change in status.

But before we got there, he pulled the car over, stopping outside a random house.

"I'm sorry," he said. "But I don't know when we'll next get a few minutes to ourselves."

His eyes dropped to my lips, and with an instant understanding, I leaned toward him.

Jason met me eagerly, and even though the kiss didn't last long, I couldn't stop the gigantic smile, which I was fairly sure would remain on my face for at least the rest of the day.

Jason laughed, giving me his own smile.

Then he drove the rest of the way to Emma's house, and seconds later, she bounded down her driveway and jumped into the back seat of the car.

"Good morning!" she said. "What's new?"

I glanced back at her, letting her see the full strength of my grin.

"There's nothing new," I answered, straightening my face as much as possible. "It's just a regular Tuesday."

"Is that so? You can't think of anything at all to tell me?"

"Nope."

"Nothing's happened since I last saw you?"

I pretended to think, bringing my finger up to my lips.

"Hmm, well, we watched a movie. Jason, I think Emma wants to hear all about The Beast Babe."

He glanced over at me, zeroing in on my finger before gently shaking his head and rolling his eyes.

I pouted. I tended to get a little silly when I was in such a good mood. Not that I could remember being in a mood that topped this one.

"The what?" Emma asked. "But no, I don't want to hear about that. Isn't there something else? Come on, Lauren, think!" She reached forward, tapping me on my head.

"Emma, stop harassing my girlfriend," Jason said.

Girlfriend! My heart soared at the word, and Jason gave me another quick glance, this time complete with a wink.

"Aww," Emma swooned, clasping her hands together, then

laughing as she switched back to normal. "Seriously though, I'm so happy for you guys, and we need to double date. I want Kai to find out the news in person, but once he knows, we can arrange something."

I looked at Jason for a reaction. "What do you think?"

I'd always liked the idea of double dating with Emma and Kai, even back when Emma was only crushing on him from afar.

"We can do that, but I was kind of hoping we'd have some time for just the two of us first. No offense, Emma."

"None taken."

"Just let me finish with getting Marina set up." He glanced at me again. "Then I promise you'll have my undivided attention."

I nodded, and I couldn't wait.

30

Jason

"ARE YOU READY TO GO PUBLIC?" I asked Lauren after parking the car in the student lot.

"Yes. I want to make sure all those girls who were after you last week know to keep their hands off."

I grinned, enjoying this possessive side of her.

"Come on, guys, I want to see Chloe's reaction," Emma said. "You should put on a show for her."

Lauren laughed. Emma and Kai had been *putting on shows* for Chloe on a regular basis while they were pretending to date.

But even though I was already getting impatient to kiss Lauren again, I would wait until I got her alone. I didn't want to be one of those couples all over each other in public.

We walked up to the school together, and I fought off the urge to grasp hold of Lauren's hand. I was confident she would have let me, but it all felt too soon, like we'd be screaming out for people to look at us.

I'd already had way too much attention lately.

Not that I really cared what anybody thought. All that

mattered was that Lauren and I were together now, and even though it had been less than twenty-four hours, I was sure we would last.

Because we already knew each other so well. I knew all her bad habits, and she knew mine.

Inside the school, everything felt the same as normal. And looking at us, no one would know anything had changed. Emma told Kai, who congratulated us, but it wasn't until I spotted Chloe in the hallway that it became my job to share the news.

After our talk in the park on Sunday, I realized exactly how much she was trying to help me. Not that I wanted it, but it still meant a lot that Chloe was so desperate for me to be happy.

"Hi guys," I said, causing Chloe to drag her eyes away from Nate and over to me.

Something about my face must have tipped her off, because she looked back at Nate. "Can you give me a minute with Jason?"

"What's it worth?" Nate asked, raising his eyebrows with a grin.

Chloe didn't rise to the bait and just swatted him away, saying, "I'll see you at lunch."

Nate left with a laugh, like he didn't mind at all.

Chloe turned to me. "What's going on? Did something happen with Lauren?"

My smile gave me away, and Chloe's mouth dropped open. She flung her arms around me, squeezing tight.

"I knew you'd find your way together." She released me. "So, what happened?"

I scratched at the back of my neck, not wanting to go into details.

"Tell me it was because of our talk on Sunday."

"Sure, that helped," I said, happy for Chloe to take credit for bringing us together, even though it was Lauren who shared her feelings first.

But I'd prompted her by asking about Emma's plan, which Chloe had made me think about, and I didn't know whether Lauren would have said anything to me if I hadn't started the conversation.

"Actually, it helped a lot. Thanks, Chloe."

She beamed at me. "So, what now? Do you have any dates planned?"

"Not yet, but I'll think of something, and Emma was saying she wanted to double—"

"Don't go on a double date!" Chloe looked horrified. "They're for people who need backup. You don't need that with Lauren. You should take her out just the two of you and do something special. Show her how important she is to you."

I nodded, not entirely sure I liked the way this was heading. I thought Chloe would be satisfied with us getting together and that it would make her back off. But it seemed she still thought I needed her help.

"Suggestion noted," I said, and it hit me that I hadn't given much thought to what dating Lauren would involve. Would she want to go out? I'd kind of thought watching movies in her room counted as dates, but maybe I needed to put in more effort.

I talked with Chloe until the bell rang, brushing off her nosier questions.

The rest of the day played out the same as any other day. I

sat next to Lauren at lunch, but other than people congratulating us, most claiming they'd always known this would happen, there wasn't much focus on our relationship, and it was only when she smiled at me that anything felt different.

It wasn't until after school and dropping Emma at home that we had a chance to talk in private again.

"So, you'll be helping your neighbor for the whole night?" Lauren asked, the disappointment already in her voice. She knew my answer.

"Sorry. I already agreed to it, before we... before there was a more enticing option."

I gave her a smile, which she returned. I'd been tempted to cancel on Marina but would have felt too guilty. She didn't have anyone else, and I'd committed to helping.

"At least we'll be together tomorrow for the road trip planning," I offered.

"That's not the same. Emma and Kai will be there."

"Oh, so you're saying you want to get me alone?" I grinned, glancing over in time to see the twinkle in her eye. I was eager to make plans with her, and as soon as I finished helping Marina, Lauren would be my main focus.

"Yes, I want to get you alone." Lauren's cheeks tinged pink, and I wished I could read her mind. "I mean, I've been waiting a long time for us to..."

"A long time? So, exactly how long have you liked me for?"

"I don't know. It was gradual."

"Since before I fake-dated Chloe?"

Lauren let out a short burst of laughter. "Way before then."

"Tell me."

She sighed. "You remember Karlie Wilkinson's pool party?"

"You're kidding?" Karlie Wilkinson moved away the summer before we started at Haven Valley High, and she threw a huge going-away party. No way had Lauren liked me for that long.

"I saw you kissing her."

I cringed. That wasn't a memory I liked to dwell on. And I wasn't the only one Karlie kissed that day. She'd brushed me aside and worked her way through a few of the other boys before the party was even over.

"I realized I was jealous," Lauren continued. "I think that was when it first started."

How was it possible that Lauren had liked me for literally years, but I had no idea?

She shifted in her seat. "How about you?"

"How long have I liked you for?"

"Yes."

I hesitated, wishing I had some romantic answer to offer. I'd liked her as a friend ever since we met in elementary school. But as more than a friend? It was impossible to pinpoint when things changed.

Maybe during the snow day in January last year? We'd had a snowball fight, and Lauren had dropped to the ground laughing. She'd looked so happy that day, and as she swept her arms and her long legs through the snow to make angels, all I could think about was how beautiful she was and how much I wanted to kiss her.

But no. That wasn't the first time I was tempted.

I shrugged. "I don't know."

"You don't know?"

"It was like you said. Gradual."

"Before Chloe?"

"Yes." I glanced over with a smile. "In fact I…"

"You what?"

I took in a breath. This didn't even matter anymore, but I wanted to be completely honest with her. "The whole thing with Chloe. She was reading a silly romance novel when we set it up, and that gave me a dumb idea."

"What idea?" The intrigue was clear in her voice, but I kept my eyes on the road ahead.

"I hoped it might make you jealous."

"I was *so* jealous," she said with a hint of sadness. "I thought I'd lost whatever tiny chance I might have had with you."

I glanced over at Lauren. "I'm sorry." The plan was supposed to make her notice me. I never intended to hurt her.

When we stopped outside Lauren's house moments later, I couldn't help myself. I took hold of her head and guided her toward me, leaning in to kiss her soft lips.

But it didn't last long before she pulled back.

"We probably shouldn't. Not until I tell my parents."

I nodded, but I wanted her to hurry up and tell them. I was sure they'd be supportive.

Lauren opened the car door, then before she got out, she turned back to me. "I almost forgot. I washed your t-shirt. Thanks for the lend, it was the perfect sleep shirt."

She opened up her backpack, retrieving the t-shirt.

"You were carrying that around with you all day?"

"Yeah. I meant to give it to you this morning so you could leave it in your car, but for some reason it slipped my mind."

She looked down at it, then she extended her arm, offering it to me.

"Why don't you keep it?" I suggested.

"Really?" She sounded awe-struck, as if I was giving her the greatest gift.

"Sure, if you want to?" The image of Lauren wearing my t-shirt—only my t-shirt—flashed into my head. "If it was perfect for sleeping in?"

She nodded. "Thanks."

Maybe it was weird, but I loved the idea of her wanting to keep it.

After looking around to make sure no one was watching, she leaned over again for a final quick kiss before leaving my car.

I watched as she ran up her driveway, and I wished I was going inside with her. But I needed to get home, do my homework, then fulfill my commitment to Marina.

After that, I intended to be the best boyfriend.

From the sounds of it, Lauren had been wanting this for even longer than I had, and I would do whatever I could to live up to her expectations.

I wouldn't waste this opportunity.

31

Jason

"ALL DONE." I collapsed backward onto the plush carpet in exaggerated exhaustion. I'd abandoned construction of the drawers last night, not wanting to keep Lauren waiting any longer. Instead, I'd finished them tonight, along with building a few other easier pieces.

Marina grinned, her eyes drifting over the twins' new bedroom. "It looks incredible." She moved next to the heap that was my body and tested the drawers. "Smooth as butter."

"Once the curtains arrive, the room will be complete."

I stood up, then glanced through the uncovered window to the bright streetlight shining outside.

"They should be here by the end of the week," Marina added, smiling at me. "I can't believe how much you got done tonight. I can unpack all the clothes tomorrow, so that'll clear some space."

The downstairs of her house hadn't changed much and was still littered with boxes.

"Oh, and I've booked the carpet installers for first thing Friday morning."

"Friday this week?" That didn't give us much time to move the boxes from the living room, and definitely not enough time to get all the painting done.

She nodded, cringing. "It'll be a rush, but it was that or waiting another week and a half… But with your help, I'm sure we can get the room emptied in time. I know it's a big ask, but if you could come over again tomorrow, that would be so helpful. I could order another pizza?"

She looked hopeful, as if expecting a bribe of pizza to seal the deal.

"I'm sorry. I already have plans tomorrow."

Her face dropped. Letting someone down had to be one of the worst feelings in the world. But I couldn't cancel on my friends tomorrow. Disappointing Lauren would be far worse.

"Why don't we get started now, though?" I said. "And I'll be here on Thursday."

"You don't mind starting now? You've already done so much tonight. Aren't you tired?"

"I'm okay."

I was tired, but the boxes wouldn't move themselves, and at least I finished my homework before coming over.

Marina led me downstairs then grabbed a craft knife from the kitchen and handed it to me.

"Why don't we open the boxes, and I'll check and see which ones need to go out to the garage. Honestly, I expect most of them will be Jordan's."

"Jordan's your brother?" I cut the packing tape away from the top of the first box.

"My little brother by fifteen minutes." She flashed me a smile before glancing over at Tommy and Alex. "Yeah, it runs in the family. So, what's in the first box?"

I lifted open the flaps of cardboard. Marina hadn't told me anything about what she was storing for Jordan, but a collection of plastic fish in all different shapes and sizes would've been pretty low on my list of guesses.

I picked up a fish, dangling it by the fine cord glued onto the top so that Marina could see from across the room.

"Oh." She laughed. "Props. That's one of Jordan's."

"Props?"

She nodded. "Jordan wants to be a filmmaker. He's made a few low-budget features, which, incredibly, some people like."

Marina shrugged as if that were hard to believe. "He's hoping to auction off most of this stuff. Trying to raise enough money for his next masterpiece."

"What type of movies does he make?" I asked, running my fingers over a giant carp.

"Monster horror."

It was the answer I'd expected. Not that there was anything monstrous or horrifying about the fish, but I'd just felt it.

"My friend—my girlfriend loves monster movies," I said, unable to withhold the smile that referring to Lauren as my girlfriend put on my face.

"You didn't mention having a girlfriend."

"It's new. Really new."

Marina smiled at my excitement, which I wasn't able to conceal at all. Then she frowned.

"And here I am, monopolizing all your time. I'm sorry, Jason. Let's crack open some more boxes while you tell me everything about her."

"Sure. Well, her name's Lauren." I used the craft knife to unseal the next box. "We've been friends since elem—"

My mouth hung open while my eyes took in the box's contents.

"What's in that one?" Marina asked.

I held up the hideous green rubber mask to show her.

"Ah, the costume box. Jordan says to protect it with my life. He thinks those masks will become valuable collector's items." She shook her head. "If they do, I'll be asking for a cut because I helped make them. The one you're holding is from a movie called The Beast from—"

"—Beneath the Deep." We finished the sentence in unison.

It was Marina's turn to look shocked. "You know it? How on earth?"

"Like I said. Lauren's a big fan. Your brother's Giordano Pacino?"

"Yes. That's his professional name. I can't believe you've heard of him. And seen his movie? I have to tell Jordan. He'll think he's famous!" She pulled her phone out of her pocket. "Not that it's a good idea to encourage him, but this will make his day, probably his entire year."

Marina typed out a message. Then she hesitated, looking back at me. "What did you think of the movie?"

My natural instinct was to be polite, but Marina didn't seem like she'd be offended by the truth, so I scrunched up my face, making her laugh.

"Would it be okay for Lauren to come over? To see the props."

"Absolutely. We could make an afternoon of it. I have a few anecdotes she might enjoy hearing, and you could even try on the costumes."

I grinned. Lauren would love that.

"Any time once all this stuff is clear,"—she swept her arm around the room—"and before Jordan's girlfriend comes to collect the things he wants to sell in Vegas."

"He's selling the props at the Mega Monster Movie Extravaganza Festival?"

"That's a mouthful. But, yeah, I guess that's the place. Are you going with your girlfriend?"

"No. We tried to get tickets, but it's sold out."

From the sympathetic smile Marina gave me, I must've looked disappointed. But she didn't know it was because I blamed myself for Lauren missing this opportunity.

"That sucks. But you know what? I'll talk to Jordan. See if he can come to collect the props himself. I know it's not the same as going to the convention, but he's always happy to talk about his movies. If you think your girlfriend would like that?"

"She'd love it. Thanks, Marina."

Lauren would flip out if she got to meet Jordan in person. It would be hard to hold the information back, but I wouldn't mention anything yet. Not until I knew for sure that Marina could set things up.

I spent another hour with her after that, opening more boxes, and then moving them into the garage while Marina made a new list on her phone of their approximate contents.

The odds of her being the sister of the Beast Babe director must have been astronomical, but the universe loved me right now, and I hoped this run of good fortune would continue.

Since last night, my jubilant mood had been off the charts, but imagining the grin on Lauren's face when I showed her the props made it soar even higher.

I couldn't wait to surprise her.

32

Lauren

EMMA WAS SETTING up her laptop on the kitchen table when the doorbell rang.

"I'll get it." I darted toward the front door before she had a chance to object.

I'd been with Emma since school ended so had missed out on those precious minutes alone with Jason in his car. And now I was excited to see him, hoping to steal a private kiss before our road trip meeting began.

But when I flung the door open, it was only Kai.

"Hey, Lauren." He greeted me with a slightly amused smile. "That was fast."

I shrugged, not wanting him to know I sprinted to the door.

"Come on in." I stepped aside, then after a quick glance outside to make sure Jason wasn't in sight, I closed the front door and followed Kai into the kitchen.

He dropped into the chair next to Emma, placing a swift kiss on her cheek and making her eyes light up.

Then we waited for Jason.

"You think I should call him?" I asked after about ten minutes.

"If you want to." Emma looked up from her laptop where she was showing Kai photos of quirky hotel rooms. "But I'm sure there's a good reason he's late."

"Maybe he forgot," I said.

"Not a chance." Kai shook his head. "He was looking forward to this."

My phone was already out on the table to make sure we didn't miss any messages, so I stared at it while I tried to decide.

I didn't want to be one of those smothering girlfriends, constantly checking up on his whereabouts. He was only ten minutes late, and this was a casual meet up, so it wasn't like it really mattered...

But then again, Jason had good manners. If he was ever running late, he would let us know. So maybe something was wrong...

Emma frowned at my expression. "Just call him if you're worried."

I exhaled, then picked up my phone.

"Hello?" Jason answered the call quickly, sounding a little out of breath.

"Hi. Where are you?" My question came out more accusatory than I intended.

There was silence for a moment.

"Crap. I'm sorry, Lauren. I didn't realize what time it was. I'll finish up here, then I'll be right over."

"Are you helping Marina again?"

Emma looked up, our eyes meeting.

"Yeah, but it—"

"You can tell me about it later. Just try not to be too long. We're all waiting." I ended the call.

"That was abrupt," Emma said. "Don't be jealous of Marina. Jason's crazy about you."

I gave her a tight smile, but it was hard to keep my jealousy in check when he was yet again choosing to spend time with her over me.

I spent all of yesterday evening alone in my room, dreaming he was with me instead of her. But he wasn't, so in the end I settled on a second attempt at watching The Beast Babe. The movie had been awesome, but I missed having Jason's arm around me while he offered up funny comments.

"I'll apologize when he gets here," I said, unable to stop the guilt. Jason was only helping his neighbor. It wasn't like there was anything going on between them, and his kind and generous nature was one of the things that made me fall for him in the first place.

The doorbell sounded sooner than I expected; Jason must have left the instant I hung up.

Just like earlier, I jumped up to answer it, opening the door and pulling him inside.

"I'm sorry," he said right away. "I lost track of time and we were trying to—"

I silenced him by holding my fingers up to his lips.

"It's okay. I'm sorry for hanging up on you. I was just feeling jealous."

"Jealous?" He raised his eyebrows as he pulled my hand away from his face, threading his fingers through mine.

I nodded, taking a glance at our entwined hands. He hadn't tried to hold my hand again since we watched the Beast

Babe, but I loved it. The feeling that we were connected. The warmth that traveled up my arm.

He lifted his free hand to my cheek, cupping it gently while looking into my eyes. "You have nothing to be jealous of. Trust me." He leaned in to give me a tender kiss, leaving me breathless.

And just like that, all my doubts faded away.

When he pulled back, he gave me an award-winning smile. "Let me convince you. Go out with me on Friday?"

"On a date?" I gazed up into his eyes. He didn't need to convince me of anything, but the thought of an actual date, just the two of us, sent an excited shiver through my body.

"Yes. A date."

"I'd love to. Where do you want to go?"

"I want to surprise you." He bit down on his lip.

"Okay." I couldn't stop the smile from spreading across my face. Jason rarely looked nervous, but he did right now, and it was too cute. Like our date really mattered to him.

He gave me another quick kiss, then walked with me back into the kitchen, dropping my hand as we entered the room.

"Sorry I'm late." Jason sat down and I took the seat next to him.

"That's okay," Emma said. "You're still helping your neighbor?"

"Yeah, she has a carpet delivery on the way, so we're trying to clear out all the boxes. Hopefully we can get the rest of them moved tomorrow."

"You're helping again tomorrow?" I asked, struggling to hide my disappointment.

He nodded, turning to look at me. "It won't be for much longer."

Emma prevented me from saying anything stupid by taking over, drawing the conversation back to the road trip. She talked us through multiple route suggestions, showing us the map she'd put together on her laptop. She'd covered the map with virtual pins, scattered across the entire country.

"So, what do you guys think?" she asked once her speech was over.

"They all sound good," Kai said with a half shrug.

Emma looked at Jason, bypassing me with a flick of her eyes. We'd already discussed things at length, and she knew I was every bit as indecisive as she was. For me, it didn't matter where we went, I just wanted to share the experience with my friends, and now with my boyfriend.

"Where was that hotel with the neon room?" Jason asked.

Emma pointed it out on the map. "You think we should go there?"

"Yeah. You sounded enthusiastic when you told me about it, and all the theming looks fun."

His words made me think of Las Vegas, and how amazing it would've been to go to the convention. Especially now we were together.

But there would be other opportunities. Other vacations with Jason, and we were planning one right now which deserved my full attention. There was no point daydreaming about the Mega Monster Movie Extravaganza Festival.

"We should definitely go there," I agreed, before looking at Emma. "We'll fight you for the neon room."

Emma narrowed her eyes, but she smiled. "May the best couple win."

I glanced over at Jason, who met my eyes with an unreadable expression. I'd basically just announced that I intended to share a room with him. It couldn't have been a surprise to anyone, and it was still months away, but the simple thought of sharing as a couple released the butterflies inside me.

With one stop on our route agreed, Emma worked around it, offering other suggestions before ultimately deciding she needed to do more research on the surrounding area. She gave us all the same research to do as homework, before waving goodbye to me and Jason, but keeping a tight hold of Kai.

33

Lauren

"DO YOU WANT TO COME IN?" I asked when Jason stopped the car outside my house.

He hesitated, making my heart drop. "We need to tell your parents."

We'd had the same conversation in the car this morning, but it wasn't like I'd even seen my parents since then. I was stalling though, worried about the almost inevitable rules that might appear. But if Jason didn't even want to come inside the house until they knew, it made my delay tactics pointless.

"You think we should do it now?" I asked.

He nodded, so I slid out of the car, waiting while Jason circled around to join me. Then I took hold of his hand, sending the warm tingles through me again, and together we walked up to the house, finding it quiet once inside.

"They must be in the basement," I said. "We shouldn't interrupt their movie."

I tugged on his hand, pulling him with me to the foot of the stairs. He didn't offer any resistance as I led him up into my bedroom and shut the door behind us.

"We need to tell them before I leave," he said in a low voice as he stepped closer to me. "I've had enough of keeping secrets for a lifetime."

I nodded. "We will. I promise."

He snaked an arm around my back, gently pulling me into him. Then he captured my lips with his, while his other hand delved into my hair. It was exactly what I wanted, and I melted into him, wondering whether his kisses would always affect me this way.

Somehow, we ended up on the bed.

"This is even better than my dream," he murmured.

"Your dream?"

He pulled back slightly with a wince, as if he regretted his words. "You know what I'm talking about, don't you?"

"Your dream from Mia's basement?"

"Yeah." He rolled away from me—not what I wanted—and put a hand over his face. "I still can't believe I did that. That I touched you without consent. I'm so sorry."

"Hey." I edged closer to him. "Don't worry about it. It wasn't your fault."

"Of course it was my fault, Lauren. I don't—"

"I was awake." I blurted my confession, unable to bear the guilt in his voice.

Jason uncovered his face and sat up, staring at me in confusion. "What do you mean? You were awake the whole time?"

I took in a breath. "I woke up, but I didn't stop you right away. I know it was wrong of me, but I'd been wanting you to touch me so badly that I just let you... I'm really sorry. Please don't feel guilty."

I bit my lip, waiting for his reaction.

"Are you serious?" His face broke out into a relieved smile. "Tell me what happened then, since you were awake. I want to know what I missed."

"What you missed?"

"Yeah. I enjoyed what you were doing in my dream, but—"

"What *I* was doing? It was about me?" I couldn't hold back my grin.

Jason smiled. "Of course it was. It was a great dream, but I think I prefer reality, especially now I know how badly you've been wanting me to touch you."

He playfully traced circles over my cheek with a finger, and I responded by thrusting my hand into his hair and roughing it up.

He laughed, then leaned down to give me a sweet, lingering kiss, before pulling away. "Thanks for telling me you woke up. I don't want to have any secrets between us."

"No secrets," I repeated.

Jason must have sensed my hesitation, because he frowned. "What aren't you telling me?"

I glanced away, unable to lie, but not sure I wanted to tell him.

"Lauren?" He sounded worried, so I knew I'd have to confess.

"I have your t-shirt."

"Yeah, I said you could keep it."

"Not that one." I pushed myself up off the bed, then walked over to pull Jason's old blue t-shirt from its drawer. I sheepishly held it up for him to see.

His eyes widened. "I was looking for that."

"You were? But you threw it out."

I'd rescued it, not stolen it. That was my story, and I was sticking with it.

"No, I was keeping it to wear for messy jobs. I can't believe you stole my t-shirt." His voice was laced with amusement. "You must have had it for almost a year?"

I nodded, giving him a nervous smile. "Do you want it back?"

"No. You can have anything of mine you want."

I grinned, then pounced, landing my body on top of his. He laughed, flipping us over, and when he kissed me again, there were fireworks.

There was an intensity there, an urgency, like he couldn't get enough of me. But it didn't last for long before the sound of my bedroom door opening interrupted us, and I froze.

Jason scrambled to separate himself from me, but he wasn't quick enough, because Mom was standing in the doorway, gaping at us.

"I didn't realize you were home," she said, recovering from the shock far quicker than I did. "Why don't you kids come downstairs? We should have a talk."

I nodded, still trying to regulate my breathing. It had been too much to hope that Mom would have backed away and let us continue.

After another quick scan of the scene in front of her, Mom turned and scurried away, no doubt going straight to gossip with Dad.

I groaned. "This isn't how I wanted to tell them."

Jason shrugged, knowing better than to say *I told you so.*

"Don't worry." He gave me a carefree smile, as if it was no big deal. Then he climbed off the bed, offering me his hand. "Come on. Let's get it over with."

Downstairs, my parents were waiting in the living room. Mom was sitting on the couch and Dad stood behind her. He didn't appear angry, but he was far from relaxed.

"So. How long has this been going on for?" His eyes darted down to our linked hands, then back up to my face. The question was clearly directed at me, not Jason.

"Only since Monday."

"And you didn't think it was something we should know about?" Dad's eyebrows bunched together.

I cringed. "I'm sorry. We were going to tell you tonight, but you were down in the basement, and we didn't want to interrupt..."

The look on his face told me that excuse wasn't going to cut it.

"I'm really sorry. I know I should have told you sooner, but I thought you'd be happy for us?"

"We are, sweetie," Mom said. "But if you expect us to allow Jason in your room with the door closed, there needs to be a level of trust. Open communication."

I nodded, swallowing the feeling of guilt, before glancing at Jason. He was maintaining a neutral expression, but he gave my hand a gentle squeeze. This sounded promising. And even though there was always the option of going to Jason's house, his mom had a habit of arriving home without warning, and it could be a little cramped. I really wanted to be able to bring him here.

"We're not naive enough to think we can stop certain things from happening. But we do expect you to be responsible."

I cringed. *Please not a sex talk right now, Mom.*

Mom noticed my expression. "But we'll discuss that later."

I nodded again. "I'm sorry for not telling you sooner."

Mom sighed and I could tell she was disappointed in me, maybe even hurt, which was worse. She stood up anyway and moved toward us. Then she wrapped her arms tight around me.

Jason let go of my hand, stepping away to give us space.

"I wish you'd told us, Lauren. But I'm so excited for you," Mom murmured into my ear. "It's about time."

I smiled, catching Dad's eye across the room. And when his own smile beamed back at me, I felt foolish for delaying the revelation. My parents loved Jason. It wasn't like I'd brought home some bad boy. He'd been a part of my life for so long, and they knew he wasn't out to break my heart.

Mom released me, then moved over to Jason. His eyes widened as she flung her arms around him, too. She whispered something in his ear, but I couldn't quite make it out.

Mom stepped back, looking at us both, appraising us as a couple, almost as if she was proud. It was the expression you'd expect to see if we were dressed up and about to go to prom.

"You should probably head home, Jason," Dad said, breaking Mom from her spell.

I gave Dad my sad face, but it didn't work. I didn't want Jason to leave yet, even if we stayed downstairs under the watchful gaze of my parents.

"I'll walk you out," Dad continued, and I frowned.

But Jason complied, giving me a reassuring smile before leaving with Dad.

I moved over to the couch where Mom was now sitting and beckoning me to join her.

"What do you think he's saying?" I muttered as I plopped down next to her.

Mom laughed instead of answering my question, then she rested her hand on my knee.

"So, this is finally happening," she said after a moment's silence. "Who made the first move?"

Heat rose to my cheeks. Talking about this was kind of private, but Mom was looking at me so expectantly, I didn't have the heart not to share at least some of the details.

"I guess I did. I told him I liked him."

"That's my girl!"

"Mom!" I whisper-yelled to shush her. I could still hear Dad and Jason talking, although I was unable to decipher their words. They'd be able to hear us, too.

Mom lowered her voice. "I'm so proud of you. That must have taken a lot of courage, even though it was obvious he felt the same. Completely besotted."

My mouth widened into an enormous smile. I couldn't help it. *Completely besotted* was an exaggeration, but what had apparently been obvious to my parents, and to Emma, was becoming clearer to me each minute I spent with Jason now we were together.

"We have a date on Friday."

"You do?" Mom clapped her hands together. "Where is he taking you?"

The sound of the front door prevented my answer, and seconds later, Dad returned.

"Well, this was all unexpected." Dad raised his eyebrows as he looked at me. "He only got rid of the fake one a week ago. My boy moves fast." He let out an almost proud chuckle.

"They have a date on Friday," Mom told him with a smile that matched my own. "And it was Lauren who put the moves on him first."

Dad laughed. "It would've been good to know that a few minutes ago."

"What did you say to him, Dad?" I asked with anguish. "You were nice, right?"

He looked affronted. "I was only making sure Jason knew to follow the rules."

"And... what are the rules?"

It was what I'd been dreading. Just because my parents were pleased with the news, it didn't mean they'd stop trying to parent us.

Dad looked at Mom, and she responded by lifting her hands up in a shrug.

"We'll figure some out," he said.

"You don't have to..." I flicked my eyes between my parents.

"Nice try, but there will be rules. And forget everything I said about wanting grandchildren. Not for at least another ten years."

I groaned, putting my head into my hands. Then I listened with amusement while my parents tried to come up with appropriate rules. But somehow, before they decided on any, the conversation switched to guessing Jason's plans for our big date. My parents had some outlandish suggestions, but they were wrong. Because Jason knew me, and whatever he was planning, it was going to be perfect.

34

Jason

I STARED at my reflection in the bedroom mirror, then used my fingers to mess up my hair. I was confident Lauren preferred it this way, and she'd no doubt mess it up even more as soon as she got her hands on me.

The guy in the mirror's lips inched up higher at the thought. He looked relaxed, self-assured, not at all how I felt. Despite planning out every detail of tonight, I was nervous.

Because tonight I was going to tell Lauren I loved her.

She probably already knew, but we hadn't said the words yet, and I was ready to take that step. I didn't want to wait.

It was insane how four days after Lauren and I confessed our feelings of like, or rather really like, my perma-smile was still there. It just wouldn't leave.

I finally caught up with Mom yesterday morning and she'd channeled her inner boa constrictor to show how excited she was about my news. I was still sore.

In the evening, I'd finished moving all the boxes into Marina's garage, which may also have contributed to the soreness, and I'd even had time to put a lick of fresh paint on one wall in her living room, all while planning out tonight.

How to make it special. What I hoped would be Lauren's dream date, at least until the day I could reveal the Beast Babe props.

And now I was ready, except for having a small errand to run.

I grabbed my phone and wrote Lauren a message.

JASON

> Looking forward to our date. I can't stop thinking about you

I cringed as I hit send. It was a bit too sappy for me, but it was true. Hopefully the message would put a smile on Lauren's face and help set the tone for tonight.

My phone battery was getting low, so I plugged it in to charge until I got back. Then I made my way out to my car, ready for the errand—buying flowers.

I wasn't sure Lauren cared about flowers in particular, but it was the gesture that mattered. And even though I already bought her chocolates—which I knew she did care about—I wanted to show I was putting in the effort.

"Jason!" Marina called out to me from across the street before I made it inside my car. She waved her cast-free arm, gesturing for me to join her.

"I'm so glad I caught you," she said as I approached. "I know it's your big date tonight. Are you leaving now?"

"No, I was just running a quick errand first. What's up?"

She smiled with relief. "I was hoping you could help me. It shouldn't take long."

"Help you with what?"

"The curtains arrived today. It would be amazing to put them up before tonight. The boys didn't sleep a wink last night because of the streetlight. I can probably manage it alone, but an extra pair of hands would be immensely helpful. You're excellent at that kind of stuff."

Marina gave me a hopeful smile while she waited for my answer.

"Okay." I probably wouldn't have time for the flowers, but I doubted Lauren would care about them once she saw the chocolates, anyway.

I followed Marina inside her house and upstairs to the boys' bedroom.

"What do you think? Fun, huh?" She tore open the packaging for the curtains, which were navy blue and decorated with cartoon pirates and other nautical drawings. "They have an extra thick lining, so they should block out all the light." Marina grinned, proud of her purchase.

"Let's see what they look like up." I reached for the box containing a wooden curtain rod, eager to get to work. But the plastic packaging didn't want to come apart in my hands.

"I'll get you my craft knife." Marina left the room, plodding down the stairs before returning a few minutes later with the knife.

After cutting the box open, I pulled out all the components and gave the instructions a cursory glance.

"We'll need the stepladder," I said.

"Of course. It's back in the garage. I'll go get it. And your toolbox is in my room."

"Thanks." While Marina went to fetch the ladder, I grabbed my toolbox and selected everything I was going to need. Then I waited for Marina to return, as all remaining hope of going flower shopping steadily evaporated.

What was taking so long? I jogged down the stairs and out to the garage where I found Marina moving things around. She pointed to the stepladder, which was trapped behind some boxes. It didn't take long for me to push them out of the way and free the ladder. Then, back upstairs, I got to work, measuring and fixing the brackets.

"It looks great." Marina stepped back to admire the new rod once I was done. "I should be able to put the curtains up on my own. I know you don't have much time."

I reached for my phone in my back pocket, momentarily panicked by its absence, until I remembered it was charging in my bedroom.

"Do you know what time it is?" I asked.

"My phone's downstairs. Oh, but I have a clock. I was hoping you could put that up too at some point. That way you can take credit for the entire room."

"Sure." I laughed, and she led me through into her room where I found the wall clock sitting on the bed next to another set of new curtains and a rod. I breathed a sigh of relief as I checked the time. "It's a lot earlier than I thought. I can put this one up now, too." I picked up the curtain rod, causing Marina to break out into a smile.

I'd be cutting it fine, but it was obvious how sleep-deprived Marina was. Having curtains might make a big difference to her catching up. And even though Lauren wouldn't be getting flowers this time, I'd at least make sure not to be late.

I wouldn't let her down again.

35

Lauren

"STILL NOTHING?" Dad asked.

"Nope." I diverted my attention away from the window and back to my phone. But Jason hadn't replied, and I'd already sent more messages than a rational person would.

"Try not to worry, sweetie." Mom walked over to where I was sitting and rested her hand on my shoulder. "You know what he's like. He probably got distracted rescuing a dog down from a tree, or helping a little old lady cross the street."

"That's right," Dad chimed in. "They're shuffling along as we speak, almost at the halfway point. He still might be a while."

Dad inched across the floor, his impression earning him a half-smile from me, but a full grin from Mom.

"And as for dogs in trees…" He made a face and shrugged.

"You knew what I meant," Mom said. "But whatever it is, I'm sure Jason's fine. Try not to worry. He'll have a good reason for being late."

"No way that boy is standing you up," Dad added.

I returned my attention to the window, staring out into the darkness. "He'll be with Marina."

"Who's that?" Mom asked.

"His new neighbor who moved in last week. He's been helping her move boxes and build furniture. Stuff like that."

"That's kind of him," Mom said.

"Yeah, but he's been spending all his time with her."

I sounded bitter. Jealous and bitter.

Mom gave my shoulder a squeeze. "He probably just lost track of time. It's easy to do when you're working hard."

I nodded. That was the most likely explanation. Except he told me wasn't helping Marina today. That tonight was just for us. And in the message he sent me earlier, he sounded excited. Not like he was about to forget me.

"What if something happened to him?" I thought out loud.

"Lauren, he's only half an hour late. There's no need to panic yet," Mom said softly. She was trying to comfort me, but somehow it had the opposite effect.

"Half an hour's a lot. This is our first date. It's a big deal. I can't believe he'd be this late without telling me. I'm going to try his phone again."

But it rang and rang. Jason didn't answer.

I stood up and paced. "What if he was in an accident? Should we call the hospital?"

"Lauren, calm down," Dad said. "Maybe his battery ran out."

"It wouldn't have rung. It would have gone straight to voicemail if the battery was dead."

I paced for a couple of minutes, blocking out my parents' attempts to calm me. My mind was racing, coming up with all sorts of crazy explanations for why Jason wasn't here, and why he wasn't answering his phone. None of them put a smile on my face.

The sense of dread was building, higher and higher, until that was all I could see in front of me. He couldn't be dead. He just couldn't. I hadn't even told him I loved him yet.

I took in a deep breath, then let it out slowly, the way my parents kept telling me to. Jason wasn't dead. He was probably just with Marina. But I couldn't wait helplessly for any longer.

"I want to go to his house. Can I borrow the car?"

Dad frowned. I could tell from my parents' expressions that they were getting worried too. Jason was too responsible, too polite to leave me hanging like this unless something was wrong, and they both knew it.

"I don't want you driving when you're upset," Dad said. "But I'll take you. Tina, you stay here and let us know right away if he shows up."

Mom nodded, taking over my position next to the window, while Dad and I darted out to the car.

DAD TRIED to reassure me on the ride over to Jason's, but I was too preoccupied with my anxious thoughts to listen.

I let out a tremendous sigh of relief as we turned onto Sunset Vista. Jason's car was in the driveway.

"Well, that's a good sign," Dad said.

He killed the engine outside of Jason's house, then reached to unbuckle his seatbelt, but I stopped him. This was something I wanted to do on my own.

"Can you wait here?" I asked, and Dad nodded reluctantly.

I jumped out of the car, then ran toward Jason's front door.

There were no lights on inside his house, but that didn't mean he wasn't there. I tried the doorbell, and when that didn't get a response, I hammered on the door.

Still no answer, and now the panic that had eased on seeing his car was building back again.

I turned around, glancing at the houses across the street. The one directly opposite had been up for sale for the longest time, but now it was occupied. Marina's house.

Jason was there. I knew it in my gut.

Wrapping my arms around myself for warmth, I stared at the house. Then, with perfect timing, Jason appeared in one of the upstairs windows.

An intense wave of relief washed over me. He was okay. He was safe. But then, almost as quickly, a new emotion took over.

In the window, Jason was adjusting the curtains. I watched as a woman approached behind him. He turned to look at her and stepped in her direction before drawing the curtains closed, blocking me from seeing anything else.

Jealousy coursed through me, and I stomped across the road without looking. Fortunately, there was no traffic, but I trusted my survival instinct would have kicked in and stopped me if there had been.

Because right now, I couldn't think. The rage was clouding my rational brain.

Reaching Marina's house, I ignored the bell and banged

my fists on the door, restraining myself from repeating the frenzied action.

No one would answer the door if they thought there was a lunatic outside.

So instead, I focused on my failing attempt to calm my breathing, waiting until the door in front of me slowly opened.

"Can I help you?" Marina furrowed her brow in a blend of concern and irritation, no doubt fueled by the crying I could hear from deeper inside her house. Jason hadn't mentioned she had children, and he'd also neglected to tell me she was drop-dead gorgeous. But I guess the reason for that was obvious.

"I'm looking for Jason. Is he here?" I already knew the answer but wanted to see whether she'd admit it.

"He's upstairs. Are you Lauren?" She still looked concerned, but her expression softened slightly.

I gave a firm nod, unsure how to react to the news that she knew who I was. That he must have mentioned me.

"Go on up." She stepped aside to let me in the house. I stormed toward the stairs, but Marina didn't follow. She'd be going to her children, and I felt a twinge of guilt that I woke them.

But there wasn't time to stop and apologize.

Because I needed to see Jason. My nerves were already in tatters from catastrophizing. But despite the relief that he was alive and well, he'd stood me up, and that filled my veins with fury.

36

Jason

LAUREN BARGED INTO THE ROOM. I looked up from my toolbox, and the moment my eyes hit hers, I knew I was in trouble.

"What's wrong?" I broke away from her glare to check the clock that was now on the wall. I wasn't late yet. We agreed I'd pick her up at seven. I was sure of it.

"What are you doing here?" she screeched, balling her hands into fists at her side. "I can't believe you're with Marina again, even though we had a date!"

My jaw dropped. I'd seen Lauren worked up on more than one occasion, but I wasn't used to her anger being targeted in my direction.

"I was just helping out." I lowered my eyebrows as concern flooded through me and I stood to face her. "So that they have curtains tonight and can get some sleep. We still have a date."

She shook her head. "You prefer her to me!"

If Lauren hadn't looked so distraught, I would've burst out laughing. It was too absurd.

"Lauren, how can you even say that? Don't you know how important you are to me?"

She shook her head again. "I'm not a priority to you."

"What?" My jaw clenched. This wasn't the right time for a declaration of love, but that she didn't know she was my number one priority stung.

"It's true," she said. "If you cared, you would be on time when we have plans, and you wouldn't have stood me up for our first date!"

"Stood you up? We said seven. No way would I ever stand you up."

She glared at me. "It's closer to eight."

My eyebrows shot up, and I took a second glance at the wall clock. Lauren followed my gaze.

"That clock is wrong," she said morosely.

I ran a hand through my hair, then scratched the back of my neck. With a new understanding of what was going on, I just needed to calm Lauren down. But she was almost impossible to reason with when like this.

"Come here." I opened my arms to her. "Let me explain."

She hesitated, but instead of letting me draw her in like she did in Mia's basement, she shook her head.

"I get it. You thought it was earlier. But that doesn't matter. If tonight was even a smidgen as important to you as it was to me, you would have made sure. You would've answered the phone when I called. You would've replied to my messages. You wouldn't have left me sitting at home, waiting. Scared you might be dead!"

"You thought I was dead?" I gawked at her. That was a massive overreaction, even for Lauren.

Tears were pooling in her eyes, so I took a step toward her, but she held up her hand to stop me.

"I don't think this is going to work." She looked away from me.

What the hell? My heart pounded. Lauren was being dramatic. She often said things she didn't mean when upset. She wasn't breaking up with me. Was she?

"Lauren, listen to me." I softened my voice in an attempt to calm her. "You're being—"

"No. I just—I thought things would be different. You put your life, our lives, on hold to help Chloe, and now it's Marina who's getting all your attention."

"Lauren—"

"Who's next? Because I doubt it'll be me."

I ached to reach out and comfort her, tell her she was wrong. But any attempt right now would only make her anger flare.

She turned on her heel without giving me a final glance and then dashed away. I wanted to chase her, but that wouldn't work with Lauren, so instead I moved to the window. I waited to hear the door slam downstairs then watched until I saw her dart across the street and disappear into her dad's car.

THE SOUND of a gentle knock on the open door broke me from my thoughts. Marina stuck her head around.

"Can I come in?"

"Sure." I forced my face into an unconvincing smile. I

hadn't moved from the bedroom, and it was her house, so I couldn't exactly say no.

"You okay?"

I tilted my head toward the wall. "Your clock's wrong. Lauren thought I stood her up."

"Oh." Marina stared at the clock, then pulled her phone out of her pocket to confirm what I already knew. "I didn't realize. I'm sorry, Jason. Did you explain?"

It should've been obvious from the way Lauren blazed out of here that my explanation hadn't been sufficient.

"I tried, but it doesn't matter. I've already been late more than once this week. Lauren doesn't think she's important to me. That I don't treat her as a priority." I sighed.

"You were late because you were helping me. I'm so sorry, Jason. This is my fault."

I shook my head, not wanting her to feel responsible for my failings.

"If she doesn't think she's important to you, you need to show her. Do something special. Make an effort that will mean something to her."

"That's what I was trying to do tonight."

"You were taking her out somewhere fancy?"

"No." I let out a dry laugh. "She wouldn't have liked that."

But now, my plan of a casual dinner at our local burger joint, followed by one of her terrible monster movies in my balloon-filled house, didn't seem like it would have been enough. Even though that was what I thought she would've wanted if asked.

Marina gave me a sympathetic smile.

"I should go home," I said.

"I wish there was something I could do to help."

"Have you heard anything from your brother about him picking up the props?"

That wasn't why I was helping Marina, but the thought of introducing Lauren to Jordan had been an extra incentive.

"Not yet. But I'll chase him."

"Thanks."

I'd been dreaming of Lauren's reaction to that surprise, and as I crossed the street back home, I wished I'd had the chance to surprise her tonight, too.

Back in my bedroom, I kicked my way through the balloons, bashing them in the air until I reached my bed and dropped onto it, drained. This wasn't how tonight was supposed to go.

Blowing up the balloons had been a waste of time. But Lauren loved balloons, and she was supposed to be here now. I briefly considered popping them but decided against it.

Because I'd make up with Lauren long before the balloons deflated.

I had to.

Tonight was only a fight, right? I'd wait for her to calm down, and then we'd talk. It was no secret Lauren sometimes had trouble controlling her emotions. But much as I hated to admit it, she had a point.

I neglected her friendship for months while I was helping Chloe, and now, just when we should have been inseparable, I was doing it again. Spending my time with Marina instead of her.

I understood the problem. All I needed was to work out a way to fix it.

37

Lauren

AS SOON AS I woke up, I rolled out of bed and plodded downstairs. I wanted to stay in bed, cozied up in Jason's t-shirt —the one he gave me—but it was more important to track down Dad.

I found him in the kitchen.

"Can I have my phone back now?" I held out my hand.

"Of course." He nodded, putting down the coffee he was cradling, before retrieving my phone from one of the kitchen drawers.

Dad had insisted I hand it over last night after I saw Jason, and I'd reluctantly complied. It was the right thing to do, because when I got worked up, I always ended up saying things I regretted.

Things I didn't mean.

Dad handed me my phone, and I held down the button to power it on.

It was hard not to think of all the stupid things I'd said to Jason. All I could do was hope and pray he'd accept my apology. And now I'd calmed down, I was anxious to talk to him.

To fix what I'd broken.

And once my messages pinged through, I'd have a good indication of how possible that would be. I was ashamed of my behavior, and I was willing to grovel for forgiveness. I'd never turned my anger on Jason like that before. What if it was too much? What if he decided it wasn't worth it? That *I* wasn't worth it.

Back in my room, I retreated into bed, snuggling under the covers while I waited with a pounding heart for my phone to spring to life.

Once it did, there were tons of notifications, all from this morning. I went straight into my message chain with Jason, hoping he'd responded in some way to the frenzied barrage of messages I'd sent while I was waiting for him.

He had, but it wasn't what I expected.

JASON

Can we talk tonight at Mia's party?

I released the breath I'd been holding. He wanted to talk. That was a good sign, wasn't it? But at Mia's party? What party?

I backed out of the conversation, wanting to check the rest of my notifications before responding to Jason. I had a missed call from Emma, along with several messages.

EMMA

Tell me Chloe's wrong!

Did you break up with Jason? What happened?

My heart sank as my eyes skimmed over her words.

Anything Chloe knew had to have come from Jason. Was he telling people we broke up?

EMMA

> Call me as soon as you get this!!!

There was also a single message from Chloe.

CHLOE

> We're invited back to Mia's tonight. Can we get ready at your house again?

A party was the last thing I was in the mood for, although right now I was in limbo. I needed to apologize to Jason, and I didn't want to wait until tonight.

So I called him. But much like last night, the phone just rang and rang.

I hated the pang of jealousy that rushed through me as I wondered why he wasn't answering. Was he with Marina again? Or maybe he just didn't want to deal with me. Either way, our talk would have to wait. So instead, I sent a message, typing out several variations before settling on my word choice.

LAUREN

> I'm so sorry about last night. I completely overreacted. Please forgive me. Call me if you get a chance, otherwise I'll see you at Mia's.

After hitting send, I kept my phone clutched in my hand. Even though he didn't answer my call, there was a chance he'd respond to a message. But after a few minutes with no sign of a reply, I accepted I'd have to wait, so I called Emma, who answered right away.

"Lauren! What happened? Did you and Jason break up?"

I hesitated, unwilling to accept that as an option. "No. We had a fight—"

"A fight? What about?"

I sighed, then shuffled to sit up. "I really messed up. I overreacted. It was all my fault."

"What happened?"

I gave Emma a recap, cringing as I recalled my behavior.

"Have you apologized?"

"I tried calling, but he didn't answer, so I sent a message. Did Jason tell Chloe we broke up?" I sucked in a breath, waiting for her answer.

"I'm not sure. She was being cagey, but she said something about getting you back together. And that it was my job to get you to Mia's party tonight. Did you hear about that?"

"Yeah, Jason said we could talk there, and Chloe already invited herself to get ready at my house."

"So you have to go."

"I guess. Unless I talk to Jason before then." I was probably dreaming, but I couldn't stop myself from hoping he'd call me sooner, he'd forgive me, and that instead of Mia's party, we'd go on our date. "I didn't even know Mia was having another party."

"Well, the rest of us weren't at the last one for long, so I guess Mia wants to try it again. Chloe said she'll be keeping it small though, the same crowd as before." Emma paused. "Don't worry about Jason. You guys will make up tonight, if not before. He already knows what you're like."

I scowled down the phone at Emma, but unsurprisingly,

since she couldn't see me, she didn't react. She was right, though. Jason knew that occasionally my mood would flare up into panic, or anger, and that hadn't stopped him from saying he liked me.

But I still felt guilty for my outburst. That Jason was always so helpful to others was one of the things I loved about him the most. It was only petty jealousy that made me hold that against him.

I sighed. "I should probably go, Em. Jason might try to call."

It was unlikely, but I was going to keep my phone glued to me for the rest of the day, just in case.

"Sure. I'll talk to Chloe and let you know what time we'll come over. I'm inviting myself too."

"I wouldn't expect anything less." I attempted a small laugh.

After saying goodbye, I slunk back under my covers. Our first few days as a couple had been incredible, and Jason wouldn't want to throw that away just because of my over-reaction.

He would forgive me.

Wouldn't he?

38

Jason

"HEY GUYS, COME ON IN." Mia stood back from the door, her eyes falling to the boxes Chloe and I had in our arms. "Is this everything, or is there more in your car?"

"This is everything," I answered.

"Should we take them straight downstairs?" Chloe asked.

Mia nodded, then walked with us down to the basement.

"Thanks so much for doing this," I said to her as I placed my box down on the floor.

"No problem. I love throwing parties, especially when I get to decorate." She gave me a warm smile. "I have to warn you though, my brother is due home from college later today. It's best if he doesn't know I have friends over, or he'll try to join in."

Chloe laughed. "You say that like it's a bad thing." She turned to me. "Don't let her worry you. Josh won't ruin anything."

Mia frowned. "With any luck he'll go out, but it was only fair to warn you. Now, why don't you show me what's in the boxes and we can get to work?"

I grinned. Mia had done an incredible job decorating for Halloween, and I couldn't wait to see what we'd be able to put together for tonight.

Chloe opened the first box, screwing her face up as she reached in and pulled out the Beast mask, before holding it up to her face. Then, with a tortured wail, she lunged for Mia, who laughed as she deftly avoided Chloe's grasp.

"That box is the costumes," I said. "We don't need it. The props are in here." I patted the big box in front of me.

"Wait, if we don't need it, why have I been lugging it around?" Chloe put her hands on her hips.

"We don't need it for decorating, but I'll use it later."

"You're planning to wear the costume, aren't you?" It sounded more like an accusation than a question, but Chloe still raised her eyebrows, waiting for an answer.

"Maybe."

I was definitely going to wear the mask. I'd attempt to squeeze into the wetsuit, too. The idea didn't thrill me, but I'd do it for Lauren.

"So, this is from an actual movie?" Mia prodded at the mask for the Beast Babe.

"Yes."

I explained how I'd unearthed it while helping Marina, and how she'd knocked on my door this morning, letting me know the exciting outcome from her conversation with Jordan. When I asked to borrow a few things so I could surprise Lauren with the news, Marina didn't even hesitate before saying yes.

I opened up the second box. "We need to be careful not to damage anything."

Marina was trusting me, and I'd sworn to protect the props, and especially the masks.

Mia nodded, then gently rummaged through the box. "Let's get out all the things we can use. Then we can decide where to put them."

We spent the next couple of hours arranging the props. Mia had an eye for design, and I was happy for her to take over.

"This looks pretty good." Chloe stood back, admiring our efforts, and I had to agree. We'd dangled the plastic fish from anywhere we could find to tie them, and we'd draped around strips of green fabric that served as a backdrop. Then we'd positioned the shredded sponges, which were supposed to be some kind of algae.

Mia shook her head. "It needs more."

"What else?" I asked. We'd already used all the props I thought would work and that hadn't looked too delicate.

"Lights. I have some green string lights that would fit perfectly with the theme."

I nodded, willing to go along with whatever Mia suggested.

"They're in the garage. Follow me."

Inside the garage, Mia waved her arm over a set of shelves that were full of neatly organized boxes. "This is all the party gear. I have balloons and streamers. Maybe we could use some of those, too?" She slid a box down to show me the contents.

"Balloons would be great," I answered. "Some of those green ones?"

"Sure." She handed the box to Chloe, who began separating out the green balloons. "And the lights are up there"—

she pointed to a box on the top shelf—"could you do the honors?"

I stretched my hands up to the box, which Mia was too short to reach, and pulled it down. Mia fished out the green lights, then I replaced the box on the shelf.

"Let's go put these up." Mia held up the lights with an excited smile before glancing at Chloe. "Bring all the balloons."

We returned to the basement, where with Mia's help, I attached the lights along the wall, while Chloe puffed out her cheeks and inflated the first balloon.

"Don't you have a pump?" she asked Mia as she tied a knot in the balloon.

"Oh, yeah, it's on the top shelf in the garage, above where the lights were. Jason, could you…"

"Sure."

I jogged up the stairs and back toward the garage. The balloon pump was easy to spot, but not as easy to reach. I jumped up, brushing against it with my fingers, edging it closer to me, until it fell down and I caught it with my other hand. At the same time, the external garage door rolled upward.

A guy ducked under the door and narrowed his eyes at me. "Who are you?" The guy's accusatory glare was intimidating, and as the door continued to roll up, I was confronted by a second set of suspicious eyes.

"I'm Jason. I'm here with Mia."

"You're dating Mia?" the first guy asked.

"No. We're just friends."

He visibly relaxed at that. "I'm Josh. Her brother." He

took a step forward then jerked his head back toward his friend. "This is Ryder."

Ryder gave me a nod.

"What are you doing with that?" Josh's eyes zeroed in on the balloon pump in my hand. But remembering Mia's comment about not wanting her brother to know she was having friends over, I hesitated.

"She's throwing a party, isn't she?"

"It's only a few people, not a real party. She's just helping me out."

"Helping you out? You mind giving me a hand with our bags and telling me all about it?" It was more of a command than a request, so I nodded, glancing at the luggage outside that the guys must have dropped before bending under the garage door.

Josh turned back to his friend. "We've got this, Ry."

"You sure?"

Josh nodded then pointed into the corner of the garage. "Those are the boxes. There's enough, right?"

"More than enough. How much stuff do you think I own?"

Josh shrugged. "Take as many as you need." He pulled his keys out of his pocket, then tossed them to Ryder. "And be careful of her. One scratch and you're dead."

Ryder laughed, apparently not intimidated by the threat. He picked up an armful of the folded cardboard boxes that Josh pointed to, before leaving us with a *thanks*.

Josh grabbed hold of two of the bags, giving me an expectant look. I abandoned the balloon pump on a low shelf, then went over to collect the other two bags from next to the open door.

"So, Mia's throwing a party to help you out?" He set the garage door into motion, waiting for it to close while he stared at me.

"Yeah, I had a—a disagreement with my girlfriend, and—"

"Your girlfriend? So you and Mia really are just friends?"

"Yeah."

Josh smiled at me for the first time, his temperament warming as he led me upstairs. He dumped one of his bags at the top of the staircase.

"That's mine. The rest are going in the room next to Mia's. Come on."

I followed him down to the end of the hallway and into the room on the right, where we piled up the bags against the wall.

"Thanks for the help," he said. "I guess I'll see you later tonight."

"You're coming to the party?" Chloe didn't seem bothered by the idea, but if there was a risk he'd somehow ruin everything like Mia thought…

"Only for a few minutes to see the old gang. I have other much more exciting plans for tonight."

Leaving Josh, I went back to the garage to collect the pump before returning to the basement.

"Did you get lost?" Chloe asked. "Look how many balloons we've done." She glanced around at the sea of balloons on the floor, smiling at the achievement.

"Sorry. I met Josh—"

"Josh's home already?" Mia sucked in her bottom lip. "Please tell me you didn't let on that I'm having people over."

I winced and held up the pump. "I was holding this, so he

guessed. But he said he had plans for tonight and would only be dropping in to see your friends."

"Oh, great. Now someone will have to restrain Allie." Mia cringed, making Chloe snicker.

I didn't know what that was about, but I didn't care. Because right now, I was too distracted by the room. With a few more balloons, it would be complete.

We'd done a fantastic job, and as I gazed around, I could picture my plan coming to life.

With the help of the pump, it didn't take long to inflate the rest of the balloons. Then, with everything all set up, and the clock ticking, it was time for me and Chloe to leave.

Mia walked us to the front door.

"At least it looks like Josh has already gone out." Mia glanced down the driveway.

"I think he's still home. He lent his car to his friend," I said.

Mia's eyes widened. "He lent his car to a friend? Are you serious?"

"Yeah. Ryder?"

"Ryder was here?" Mia looked a little flustered, but she quickly regained composure.

"Yeah. We took his bags to the room next to yours. Looks like he's staying a while."

"Really?" Her voice squeaked a little.

I nodded, amused by her reaction to the news. Mia had always come across as super calm and confident, so this was new.

Chloe laughed and took hold of my arm. "Let's go. I need to go home and eat before you take me to Lauren's."

Back in my car, Chloe turned to me with a grin. "I can't wait to see Lauren's face. She's going to love this."

I hoped she was right. "You promise not to tell her what's going on?"

"I can keep a secret. You know that."

I nodded. "I want to surprise her."

"You will, I'm sure of it."

"Thanks for your help today, Chloe."

"No. Thank you for calling me. I didn't do a lot, but you know I'm always here for you. I want to help."

I gave her a heartfelt smile. "Thank you."

My excitement was growing fast. Even though I kept needing to push down the nagging guilt that I hadn't called Lauren to make up, waiting a few hours longer and surprising her would be worth it.

Tonight I was going to let Lauren know how important she was to me. Everything was falling into place, and now, all I had to do was wait.

39

Lauren

JASON'S CAR was already here. It was the first thing I noticed when we arrived outside Mia's house. I tried to act normal, to hide my nerves as we all piled out of Kai's car.

Emma and Chloe insisting on getting ready at my house had been pointless. I hadn't been in the mood for conversation, and since my own preparations took less than five minutes, I spent most of the time impatiently watching Chloe do her makeup.

Although, after last time, I couldn't help but wonder if she was being deliberately slow. And from the way she rushed to gather up her things after her phone chimed with a new message, I suspected I was right. It was some kind of delay tactic.

Mia greeted us at her front door then led us through to the kitchen where Nate and Allie were talking. Chloe went straight for Nate, and he wrapped his arm around her, while Mia came to stand next to me and lowered her voice.

"Jason's already in the basement. He wants to talk to you

in private before the rest of us go down." She gave me a hopeful smile. "I promise not to lock you in again."

"Thanks." I returned her smile, then left to see Jason. I'd been waiting for this moment, and now it was finally here, the nerves were out and my heart was pounding.

It had to be good news. It was impossible to believe Jason would want to talk to me here, like this, if he wanted to break up. He could never be that cruel.

But that he hadn't just called and put me out of my misery was confusing. There had to be something else going on, and the suspense had been building all day.

With a tentative pull, I opened the door to the basement. Then, step by step, I descended, my eyes widening in wonder as I took in the sight in front of me.

Jason had completely transformed the basement. The overhead lights were off, and instead, a green hue was being cast over the room from a singular string of bright bulbs.

It was themed as if underwater, almost swamp-like, with murky green sheets and aquatic ornaments scattered around.

My grin broke out as I took the last step down. Jason did this for me, and if he'd been trying to recreate the set of The Beast Babe, it was spot on. The whole creepy atmosphere blew my mind.

"Jason?" I called out eagerly. He was supposed to be down here, but other than the gentle lull of ocean wave sound effects coming from the speakers, it was silent. "Are you here?"

My eyes sketched around the room as I waded forward through the balloons on the ground. Without warning, a loud gurgle erupted from the darkest corner of the room, and a shape emerged from the shadows.

My jaw dropped almost to the floor as the shape, the Beast

from Beneath the Deep, approached with its arms outstretched.

"Jason?" I couldn't believe what I was seeing.

The beast gurgled again and moved closer. I stared at it, taking in all the details. It looked exactly the same as the creature from The Beast Babe, the costume having undergone several improvements since the first movie. But this was too accurate, too impressive to be anything other than the real deal.

"How did you..." I shook my head in awe.

Once he was close enough to touch, the Beast—Jason—stopped moving.

I reached up to put my hands on his mask, stroking over its flexible rubber gills before gently pulling it up and off. Jason let out a slow breath as his eyes locked onto mine.

"What's going on?"

He gave me a nervous smile. "I wanted to surprise you."

"You did. Where did you get the costume?" My eyes slid down his body, then back up, before settling on the mask in my hand.

"I called in a favor."

"A favor?" I glanced around the room again.

"Do you like it?" he asked.

I nodded. "It's incredible. But I don't understand..."

"I wanted to do something for you. Make an effort. What you said last night—"

"I'm so sorry," I interrupted. "I completely overreacted, and I didn't—"

"Lauren." He picked up my free hand with both of his. "It's okay. I understand why you were upset, disappointed in me."

I opened my mouth to argue, but Jason powered on. "You were right, and I'm sorry. I wasn't acting like you were a priority, but you are. And going forward, I'm going to prove it to you."

I shook my head before letting the words rush out. "You don't have to prove anything. I love the way you help other people. I was being selfish because I want you all to myself." Jason's lips curved up into a smile at that. "I'm so sorry I flipped out and ruined our first date."

"We can still have a first date. It'll just be a different one."

I nodded, but I was curious. "What did I miss? Tell me what you had planned."

He shrugged. "It wasn't much. I thought you'd prefer to keep things low-key. So I was going to take you to Jimmy's for burgers, then back to my house to watch one of your terrible movies. I got you your favorite chocolates too, so they could be our movie snack, assuming you would have shared?" I nodded with a grin. Jason had just described my perfect date. "Oh, and then after the movie, I was going to tell you I love you."

"What?" The sound escaped me as a whisper. He'd dropped that admission so casually.

"I love you," he repeated, gazing deep into my eyes.

My heart somersaulted, and I flung my arms around him, almost knocking him over.

"Whoa, careful of the costume." He laughed.

"Sorry." I loosened my hold on him and pulled away so I could see his face. I took a deep breath. "I love you too."

His eyes lit up at my words and he drew me back into him. This time, our lips collided, and Jason kissed me like we'd been apart for months.

This was it. Everything I always wanted was finally happening.

He loves me.

"We should let the others down," Jason said once our kiss slowed to a stop. He brushed his fingers over my cheek.

"Oh, yeah, I guess."

I'd forgotten all about our friends.

"I'm dying to get changed, but my death will probably be at Chloe's hands if I don't let her see me first."

I laughed. "Should I go get them?"

"Yeah, thanks." Jason stretched the mask back over his face.

I took a step back, taking in the vision of the Beast again. I had so many questions about how this was possible, but for now, I had a job to do. So, after a quick glance back at Jason, I bounced up the stairs out of the basement, then rejoined our friends who were still in the kitchen.

They all turned to look at me, but instead of showing my grin, I forced my lips into a straight line.

"I think there's something in your basement," I said to Mia.

"Are you serious?" She widened her eyes in exaggerated fear. I still didn't know Mia that well, but I liked that she was playing along. She was obviously in on Jason's plan, but I wasn't sure how much everyone else knew.

"Yeah. Some kind of sea creature. It was hideous."

Mia frowned. "Maybe we should send the guys down first, to make sure it's safe, or in case the creature is hungry?"

Chloe laughed and took hold of Nate's hand. "Good plan. Come on, Nate. Let's go check it out."

Nate puffed out his chest, but I didn't miss the fake look of panic he shot Kai. "You coming too?"

"No way," Emma answered on Kai's behalf. "I'm not letting you feed him to a sea monster." She took hold of Kai's arm, then crossed her other arm over his chest in a protective stance.

Kai grinned. "Sorry, bro. You'll have to fight it alone."

Chloe yanked on Nate's hand, and he willingly went with her. Then, despite Emma's initial protest, the others followed along too. We moved as a group, all playing up the fear aspect and letting Chloe be our brave leader.

"Hello?" Chloe called down into the basement. "I brought you dinner!" She gave Nate a push, but he didn't budge. Instead, he scooped Chloe up into his arms, then slowly descended the stairs.

40

Jason

"PUT ME DOWN, YOU NEANDERTHAL!" Chloe couldn't stop her giggles while she clawed at Nate's arm, and it was a struggle to hide my own amusement as I watched my friends head down the stairs.

But, playing my part, I moved out from my dark corner, roaring at the top of my lungs.

Allie let out a small yelp, and Emma jumped, but everyone else just laughed before approaching me with curiosity. After a minute or two of prodding, their interest waned, so I pulled the suffocating mask back off.

"You're going to get changed now?" Lauren almost looked disappointed. But after squeezing myself into the wetsuit, I couldn't wait to be free.

"Yeah, I'll be right back."

Mia gave me a concerned glance. "Will you be able to…?"

She helped me do up the costume earlier, mostly down to the embellishments that obstructed the zipper at the back.

"Actually, I could use a hand."

I let my eyes drift back to Lauren and she jumped at the opportunity.

"I'll help. Where are your clothes?"

"They're in the bathroom." I took hold of Lauren's hand, leading her with me, dropping the mask back into the box where it belonged on the way.

Inside the bathroom, I switched on the light, then I locked the door.

Lauren gave me an almost shy smile. "So, here we are again."

I nodded, amazed how much things had changed in little over a week. Changed for the better.

"Help me out of this, will you?" I turned my back to her, and she reached up to find the end of the zipper. She slowly lowered it, carefully clearing a path through the decorations as she unzipped.

"Did Mia help you put this on?"

"Yeah, but without her I'd still be struggling, and you'd still be waiting for Chloe to paint her face." I glanced at her over my shoulder. "Don't tell me you're jealous? She only helped with the zipper."

She shook her head. "I'm not going to be jealous anymore."

"You're not?" I grinned.

"No. At least I'll try not to be. I trust you, Jason, and I won't do anything to mess this up."

I nodded as I turned away from her again. Lauren's words meant a lot, even though controlling her emotions wouldn't be easy. But I'd play my part too. I wouldn't give her any reason to doubt me.

Lauren finished unzipping the wetsuit, and once it was

loose, I pulled my arms out and turned to face her. "I think I can handle it from here."

She frowned. "You want me to leave?"

"You want to stay?"

"Well, I kind of thought we should stay in here for at least seven minutes. For old times' sake." She dropped her eyes to my chest, and I laughed.

"Sure, but I want to take this off before I damage it."

Lauren nodded and turned to face the wall, giving me at least the illusion of privacy.

"Eyes closed," I said, before leaning around her to check she was following the order. Then, with limited space, I worked on separating my legs from the wetsuit.

"You didn't explain how you got the costume," Lauren said. "It looks like the real thing."

"It is."

"Really?"

"Yeah. I found it when I was helping Marina move some boxes."

"Marina had it?" The confusion was apparent in her voice.

"It turns out Giordano is her brother."

"You're kidding?" She twisted her neck to look at me, locking her eyes onto mine. With a smile, I reached out and turned her head back to face the tiled wall.

"It's true."

"So, Marina let you borrow the costume?"

"Yeah, and all the props."

"Wow."

Talking about this now, I remembered I still hadn't told Lauren the best part. I'd been so focused on making up, on telling her how I felt, that I hadn't given her the main surprise.

"We had an idea." I finished stripping the wetsuit away from my skin. "I was going to invite you to Marina's to see everything, and she was trying to arrange it so that Jordan— that's Giordano to his fans—would be there at the same time. I thought you'd get a kick out of meeting him." I grabbed my jeans from the pile of clothes I'd left on the floor, then pulled them on.

"That would be amazing," Lauren answered while I threw on my t-shirt.

"You can look now."

She swung around, dazzling me with her warm smile.

"Unfortunately…" I started, and Lauren's smile dropped a bit. "Marina wasn't able to get it set up. She hoped Jordan would visit to collect his props. But he doesn't have time, so his girlfriend is getting them instead. They're taking them to the convention in Vegas to auction them off."

"That's okay. It would have been fun to meet him, but this, what you did out there, it's awesome."

"Well, actually you'll still be able to meet him." I braced myself, preparing for the explosion.

"What do you mean?"

"It turns out that Marina really appreciated my help with her house, and she wanted to repay the favor. And since she couldn't get Jordan to come to us…"

Lauren's expression stayed blank, as if she wasn't sure she was correctly interpreting my words, but I could see the excitement growing in her eyes.

"She arranged for Jordan to get us tickets," I said.

"Tickets?"

"To the Mega Monster Movie Extravaganza Festival," I confirmed.

Lauren squealed, flinging her arms around me for the second time tonight. "Are you serious? We're going to the festival?"

I grinned, then tilted her head back so I could gaze into her beautiful caramel eyes. "We're going to the festival."

Lauren pulled down on my neck, bringing my face close to hers so that she could shower me with enthusiastic kisses. "I can't believe this, Jason. You're incredible. We're going to have the best time! I love you so much!"

"Did I mention they're VIP tickets?"

"No!" She tightened her embrace, and I was half expecting her to lift me off the floor.

This was Lauren at her happiest, and the joy was almost overwhelming.

"We should go back outside," I said with a laugh.

"Before our seven minutes are up?"

"Well, it's not like we're re-enacting things accurately. If we were…" I reached out to flip the light off, plunging us into darkness. "It would be seven minutes in the dark."

"I like the way you think." Lauren lowered her voice. She reached for me, landing her hand on my t-shirt, then she traced over my chest with her fingertips. "Do you remember what you said when we were in here before?"

"I said a lot of things."

"You said if I was in here with a guy I liked that I'd be mauling him. That I was an animal."

"Was I wrong?" I teased, hoping I could somehow encourage her.

She laughed. "You're about to find out."

"Oh yeah?" And then, because I couldn't resist, I added, "Go for it."

Lauren laughed, and I hoped I'd be able to hear that sound —my favorite—every day. She didn't attack me, though. Instead, she trailed her hand up my body, and when she reached my face, she stroked her fingers across my skin.

This could be a dream, but I knew it was real. All my senses were wide awake, and I felt so alive.

Lauren slipped her hand into my hair, ruffling it with her fingers, before guiding my head down until our lips met.

And then, for what had to be more than seven minutes, we shared a kiss that was tender, loving, and something that I wanted to keep on sharing with Lauren, my best friend—my girlfriend—forever.

BOOKS BY KENZIE

Summer Expectations

Kisses and Castles (Ava & Colton)

Haven Valley High

Faking What's Real (Emma & Kai)

Challenging What's Real (Chloe & Nate)

Sharing What's Real (Lauren & Jason)

Celebrating What's Real (Mia & Ryder)

Resisting What's Real (Allie & Josh)

For more information on current and future releases visit
kenziebrayne.com

Plus, get updates and exclusive bonus content when you sign up at
kenziebrayne.com/newsletter

WILL HE SAY YES TO A MISTLETOE KISS?

Ryder

When family drama leaves me homeless for winter break, crashing with my best friend, Josh, is the obvious solution.

I'm staying in the room next to his sister, Mia, with only a shared bathroom between us.

Luckily, we get along great—maybe better than we should—and as we spend more time together, I can't stop my feelings from growing.

But Josh has rules around Mia, and even though I'm tempted, I won't betray his trust.

Mia

All I wanted was for my parents to come home and watch me dance in Santa's Showcase.

A sprained ankle dashes my hopes, leaving me housebound. At least I'm not alone.

And after secretly crushing on Ryder for years, I love having him so close by. He's keeping me entertained, cooking feasts, and showing me he cares.

Ryder says I'm off-limits, but when I find out my feelings aren't one-sided, I'm ready to celebrate.

I won't let Josh stand in our way.

ABOUT THE AUTHOR

A lifelong lover of story, Kenzie originally studied storytelling through film, before turning her attention to the written word. She loves to read and write romance with kind heroes, crushes, awkward moments, temptation, and heart-pounding new experiences.

Made in the USA
Columbia, SC
16 June 2025

59495949R00148